NOT ANOTHER MANWHORE

Not Another Romance Novel

R.L. KENDERSON

Not Another Manwhore

Chapter One

BREE

I CURLED my lip in disgust as the man across the restaurant got down on one knee and proposed to his girlfriend.

"What's up with Bree?" Alexis asked the rest of our friends sitting around the table as she caught me staring.

I discreetly pointed to the couple, and my friends all turned to look.

"Don't be so obvious," I hissed.

Pru looked over her shoulder at me. "The dude is proposing in a restaurant. He *wants* everyone to look."

I scanned the room. Sure enough, we weren't the only people watching. "Yeah, I suppose you're right."

The woman was standing now with her hands to her mouth. The man's back was to me, but I could just imagine what he was saying. Something about not wanting to spend another day without her and loving her for the rest of their lives and yada, yada, yada.

I rolled my eyes.

The woman nodded, and the room erupted in applause.

I picked up my wineglass and took more than a sip.

"Barf," I said.

Paisley got a wistful look on her face. "I think it's sweet."

"You would," Alexis joked, and we all started laughing.

Tonight was the monthly dinner I had with my six friends from high school. Tessa, Paisley, Alexis, Pru, Elizabeth, Isabelle, and I had been in choir together since we were freshmen in high school, which was funny because none of us had gone on to do a single thing with singing once we graduated.

And while I saw many of my friends outside of our regular meetup, it was hard for all of us to be in the same place at the same time. Because of this, we made our scheduled get-togethers months in advance. Every fourth Wednesday was reserved for us.

"Okay, Bree, what gives?" Tessa asked. "You seem extra salty tonight."

Alexis nodded. "Yeah, I mean, we're the unofficial She-Woman Man-Haters Club, but you seem a little more..."

"Hateful," Paisley finished.

Isabelle wrinkled her nose. "Since when did we name ourselves the She-Woman Man-Haters Club?"

I shook my head in mock sadness. "You poor thing."

"What?" Isabelle asked as she looked around at us.

Isabelle had had a strict mom, growing up, and she

hardly ever got to watch movies or television. She'd even had to lie about what she watched whenever she hung out at one of our houses.

"It's from *The Little Rascals*. They have a club called the He-Man Woman-Haters Club," I explained.

Alexis smiled. "I'm glad someone got my joke."

"I loved that movie when I was little," Paisley said. "My brother, sister, and I would watch it all the time."

"I think we need a better name for our little group," Pru said.

I raised my glass. "How about Men Suck?"

It came out a little too loudly, and the guy at the table next to us looked over at us with a frown.

Paisley snorted her laughter and hid her mouth behind her napkin.

"Don't mind her," Elizabeth said about me. "She got cheated on. Again."

The man next to us nodded and turned back to his date.

"You don't have to tell everyone," I pointed out.

Elizabeth shrugged. "Why? It's nothing to be embarrassed about."

"Yeah, right," I muttered under my breath.

What's the old saying?

Fool me once, shame on you. Fool me twice, shame on me.

That's it.

Except for me, it was more like *fool me three times, give up on men.* I'd had four serious relationships since high school, and three of my boyfriends had cheated on me. And the other? Yeah, he'd decided he liked men better than women, so there you go.

I was beginning to think there was something wrong with me. In the end, I was the common denominator in all these relationships.

Thankfully, I had my friends. They were all single or divorced with a host of bad affairs behind them. Some time ago, we'd decided to embrace our solo lifestyles and just say no to men. We didn't need them if we had each other.

"You're not responsible for others' actions, Bree. Only your own," Elizabeth said. "But Tessa's right. You do seem more upset tonight. Did something happen with the ex?"

"No," I said with a sigh. "My cousin's wedding is a little over a week away. It's from Thursday to Sunday, which means, for four days, I will have to hear about how I'm the only single person in my whole family."

"Holy crap." Paisley's eyes went wide as she took a commiserating sip of her wine. "How is a wedding that many days?"

"My cousin's fiancé has money. We're going to a lake resort. The groom rented out all the cabins for the wedding party. The place also has a hotel, and he rented the whole thing out for the guests. I don't even think all the rooms are booked."

Alexis whistled in amazement. "My ex-husband wouldn't even pay for our own hotel room he was so cheap. We had to go home and sleep in our own bed on our wedding night."

Tessa sipped her wine and looked about as disgusted as I had when I saw the couple getting engaged. She had a thing about rich people and had never really liked Alexis's ex even though his family was more comfortable than rich. Not that I blamed her.

I set my glass down and leaned my arms on the table, feeling a bit defeated by the whole wedding situation. "If it were anyone else's wedding, I would be excited. My cousin's getting married on the beach at sunset, and I get to take two days off of work. It would be fun. But *my mother* is going to be there..."

I was an only child, and my mom was constantly asking when I was going to get married. She was the oldest of five girls, and she was so embarrassed her daughter didn't have a husband yet. After my cousin was married, it would be only me and Kylie left. As the youngest cousin, Kylie was only seventeen.

I was on my own next weekend.

"How did she take your last breakup?" Tessa asked.

I sighed. "She doesn't get it. I told her I caught Rick in bed with another woman. You know what she told me?"

Everyone shook their heads.

"That I can't be so picky."

"Ouch," Pru said.

"Yeah. I told her I'd rather die alone than be with a cheater." I shook my head sadly. "She doesn't get it though. She thinks because my dad cheated that all guys do. She doesn't understand that there are some actual good men out there who are faithful."

"They all just happen to be taken or haven't been born yet," Pru said dryly.

"Exactly," I agreed.

Paisley lifted a shoulder. "Take a fake boyfriend."

Isabelle's eyes lit up. "That's a good idea."

I raised my eyebrows in horror. "No way. Too complicated. Plus, I don't even know anyone to take."

"Is there someone from work?" Paisley asked.

"No. And even if there were, that would be too awkward."

"Tessa," a voice called out, and the seven of us turned our heads.

"Whoa," Paisley said in a low voice. "Someone hold my underwear."

Tessa whipped her head around. "*Ew.* That's my brother."

"He's still hot," Paisley pointed out with a shrug.

Paisley wasn't wrong. Tessa's brother, with his thick and dark hair and tempting teal-blue eyes, was hot as sin. To top it off, he had a short beard, and his left arm was covered in tattoos. I was a sucker for beards and tattoos.

I quickly picked up my wine and took a long drink.

"Hey, Zack," Tessa said when her brother reached us. She looked at the pretty woman on her brother's arm. "On a date?"

Zack smiled. "Tessa, this is Kim. Kim, this is my sister, Tessa."

Kim smiled and put her hand up in a small wave.

Zack scanned the rest of us and stopped when he reached me. "Kim, these are my sister's friends."

I looked away from Zack. "Hi," I said to Kim, as did my friends.

Tessa and Zack had gone to private school until Tessa transferred to our public high school. Zack had stayed where he was, so because of this, I—and the rest of my friends—didn't know him that well. He had always been off, doing his own thing with his own friends in high school even though he was only two years older than us.

I peeked at Zack out of the corner of my eye to see if he was still looking at me, but he had turned his gaze to his date. It was a relief and a disappointment, but I didn't let myself think about those feelings.

A few minutes later, Zack said good-bye, and then he and his date left.

"Is Kim your brother's girlfriend?" Alexis asked.

Tessa laughed. "Uh...no. My brother is a manwhore. I don't think he knows what a girlfriend is."

"Ooh, Bree, you should take Zack as your date to the wedding," Paisley said.

I had just taken a bite of my dinner, and I almost choked on it. Pounding my chest a couple of times, I shook my head. "I don't think so. Dating men who can't keep it in their pants is why I'm single as it is."

"But this wouldn't be a real date," Paisley said. "It's just so your mother will leave you alone."

I tried to picture Zack with my family. I was sure my mother would love him.

And that would be if Zack even said yes.

Nah. Not worth it.

"I think I'll pass."

"Good decision," Tessa said. "Zack is handsome and charming, but you can do better."

I laughed. "You're such a nice sister."

She tilted her head and grinned. "I know."

"So, if we're not going to help Bree find a date for the wedding, then we should discuss our 'club' name," Pru said, using finger quotes. "We've been doing these monthly dinners for a couple years. It would be fun to give ourselves a title."

"I'm game, and I already said my idea."

Paisley tapped her chin. "How about Single Ladies?"

"That's a song," Tessa said. "What about The Spinsters Club?"

"That term is antiquated and sexist," Pru said. "Plus, it technically means, never married, and Alexis has been divorced."

"Thanks for thinking of me," Alexis said.

Pru picked up her glass. "Always."

"Vibrators Forever," Alexis said with a laugh, and Pru almost spit out her sip of wine.

"Hey, I still like sex," Paisley said. And she did. In fact, she liked it a little too much and often got sexually involved with men who wanted to keep things casual...but then she would fall in love and get her heart broken when the guy didn't want to get serious.

"How about No More Bad Dates?" Elizabeth offered.

Isabelle pursed her lips, and then her eyes went wide. "How about Not Another Romance?"

I smiled at my friends. "I don't think it matters what we're called. As long as we're united single ladies with our vibrators so that we never have another bad date or experience romance again."

"You forgot She-Woman Man-Haters and Men Suck," Alexis said with a laugh, bringing up the two names we'd said earlier.

"Right." I picked up my wine and held it out. "Here's to United She-Woman Single Ladies with Our Vibrators So We Never Have Another Bad Date or Experience Romance Again Because Men Suck Club."

My friends picked up their glasses as well, and we clinked our drinks together.

"Hear, hear," Pru said, and we all laughed at our ridiculously long name. "But I think Isabelle's idea was shorter."

"*And,*" Paisley added, "*I* think we still need to find you a date for the wedding."

God, no. That was never going to happen.

Chapter Two

BREE

THE NEXT MORNING, my phone rang as I was getting ready for work.

"Hello, Mom," I said when I answered.

"Good morning."

"Morning." I put my phone on speaker, so I could finish putting on my makeup.

"I'm headed over to your aunt's house this morning."

I sighed. I knew where this was headed. She didn't even have to tell me which aunt she was referring to.

"Oh?" was my only response.

"Yeah, I'm helping with the wedding plans. I figure I don't have anything else to do."

Yeah, I got the message. She could be helping me with my wedding plans if I were getting married.

"Sounds fun," I said as I put on my mascara.

"Why don't you join us?"

"Because I have to work. It's Thursday."

"Well, Tina's not working."

I looked down at my phone. "It's Tina's wedding."

"I know. I just—"

"No, Mom."

"No what?"

"Just no. Whatever it is you're going to say, no."

"Why did you break up with Rick again?"

Really? "He cheated on me."

"Honey, men stray. It's not a reason to let go of a good man."

I clenched my fists and bared my teeth. "Mom, it might have been fine for you, but it's not for me. I deserve better."

"Don't say that about your father—may he rest in peace."

He had been an okay dad, but he had been a shitty husband, and I had no plans to take back my words.

"Is there something else I can help you with?" I asked. I was about done with this conversation.

"What, I need a reason to speak to my daughter?"

Here comes the guilt trip.

"No, but I really do need to finish getting ready for work."

"If you had a husband, you wouldn't have to work."

I groaned. Never mind that I wanted to work, husband or no husband.

"Maybe you'll meet someone at the wedding."

My ears were ringing now. So, now, I was going to

spend next weekend hearing about why I was single while she tried to set me up with every single guy from eighteen to sixty.

I couldn't handle it.

"I already met someone," I blurted out as my conversation with my friends from the night before ran through my head.

My mother gasped. "You did? Why didn't you say so?"

Because it's a lie. "Because it's new."

"Oh, I'm so happy. I can't wait to tell everyone."

Oh no, what have I done? "Mom, wait. It's still new, and—"

"Hogwash. Everyone's going to meet him anyway."

I couldn't argue with her logic. "But—"

"What's his name?"

"His name?"

My mom laughed. "Yes, honey. What's his name?"

My mind raced as I tried to think of something, and an image of Tessa's brother popped into my head. "Zack," I said before I really thought about it.

"Zack. Zack. Why does that sound familiar?"

"I have no idea."

"Isn't that Tessa's brother?"

"How would you know that?" I asked, shocked that she knew that.

"I ran into Tessa and her brother one day. He's a very handsome man, Bree."

Shit, shit, shit. My question made it sound like an omission.

I was going to have to come clean about the whole thing. Maybe she'd get so mad at me that she wouldn't speak to me all weekend.

That wasn't fair. Despite everything, I did love her.

I sighed. "Mom, look—"

"I have to run, and you need to get to work. But don't worry. By next weekend, everyone will know you have a new man in your life and that you're just as good as your cousins."

What the hell? I'm not as good as my cousins because I'm single?

Now, I was angry.

"Yeah, you do that," I barked and ended the call without waiting for her to speak.

I looked up into the mirror at my half-finished face and shook my head. "Way to go, Bree. Now, you have to ask Zack to go to a wedding with you."

It was a good thing he was handsome and charming. If I could get him to agree, maybe Paisley's idea would work after all.

I finished my makeup and picked up my phone.

"Hello?"

"Hey, Tessa."

"Hey. What's wrong?" she asked.

"Remember last night, how we talked about me bringing a date to the wedding?"

"Yeah," she said hesitantly.

"Well...I kind of need to ask your brother an important question."

"You didn't..."

"I did. My mother just wouldn't leave me alone."

I heard Tessa sigh. "Okay, I'll get you in touch with him...but be careful."

I laughed at her concern. "I'm taking him as a date. I'm not going to fall in love."

Chapter Three

ZACK

I TOOK a bite of my sandwich and rested my arms on the side of my work truck bed as I watched an unfamiliar black sedan pull up in front of the house I was working on. I'd been installing electrical work there since six that morning, and I was past due for a break.

My sister had asked where I would be around lunch, but that wasn't her car.

The driver's side opened, and Bree Keller, my sister's friend, got out of the vehicle.

I frowned as she neared, and I stepped away from my truck.

She smiled hesitantly. "Hi, Zack."

"Is everything okay with Tessa?"

Bree tilted her head in question. "Didn't she tell you I was stopping by?"

"No."

"Oh, I thought she told you I was coming."

"She didn't." Bree still hadn't answered my question. "Is Tessa okay?"

"Yes, she's fine."

Now that the worry was gone, curiosity took over, and I wondered why she had come to see me. I eyed Bree from her head to foot.

Back in high school, I had seen her around. She'd been cute back then, but she was two years younger than me, and I'd had plenty of girls my own age to keep me occupied.

Now, she was smoking hot with a rocking body, even wearing what looked to be her work clothes. She was about half a foot shorter than my six-one with light-brown hair and fair skin and a sprinkling of freckles across the bridge of her nose. The other night at the restaurant, she hadn't looked so formal with her dark lipstick, and I could still picture her low-cut shirt, showing off an impressive set of tits.

I resumed my position behind my truck before she saw my dick getting hard. He didn't understand that Bree wasn't there to see him.

"What's up?" I asked, picking up my water bottle and taking a long drink in hopes it would cool me down.

The lip Bree was chewing on slid out of her mouth. "I need a favor."

My eyes widened. "From me?"

Even though she was my sister's friend, I didn't know her that well. We'd gone to different high schools, and I'd moved out as soon as I graduated. The most time I could ever remember spending with her was the afternoon my mom had forced me to drive Tessa and two of her friends to the movies. None of them had said a single word to me the whole time. I didn't think I'd even gotten a thank-you.

Maybe I should tell her she already owes me one.

"Yes, from you." She looked away, and her eyes landed on the back of my truck bed. "You're an electrician, right?"

I sighed. I didn't understand why everyone and their dog thought I should help them with a large discount—or even worse, for free. I didn't mind helping my friends with projects in their houses, but when my friend's neighbor's nephew started coming around, my annoyance began to rise.

The good thing was, my budding erection was gone.

"Are you building or remodeling?" I asked.

Because I loved my sister, I'd give Bree advice, but I wasn't going to work for nothing.

"Huh?"

"Are you building a new house or remodeling an old one?" I said a little slower.

Her forehead wrinkled. "Neither." A second later, the area between her eyebrows smoothed out, and she laughed. "Oh. No, I'm not doing either. My favor has nothing to do with you being an electrician."

Interesting. "Okay then, what can I help you with?"

She opened her mouth, but no words came out.

I lifted my brow in question and shoved my last bite of food in my mouth. "It can't be that bad," I said after I swallowed.

"It's embarrassing."

The plot thickens. "If I promise not to laugh, would that help?"

This made her smile, and I hoped I'd eased her mind a little.

"What are you doing next weekend?"

"Are you asking me out on a date?"

"No. I mean, yes." She sighed. "I mean, it's more complicated than that."

I glanced at my watch. The homeowners weren't around, but I still needed to get back to work. I had plans later that evening, and I wanted to be finished up with the wall I was currently wiring.

"I don't mean to be rude, but I need to get back in there." I jabbed my thumb at the house behind me.

"Right. Yeah, I need to get back to work too. I'm on my lunch break."

"So..." I prompted.

"I need a date to my cousin's wedding so that my mother won't harass me all weekend about why I don't have a boyfriend."

"Uh...listen, Bree, I don't go to weddings with women I'm fucking, much less with someone I'm not."

Wrong impressions were had all around when one went with someone to a wedding. Like thoughts of their own nuptials.

My eye twitched at the thought.

"No, I don't want you to be my real date. I want you to be my fake date."

I hadn't expected that. "You want me to be your fake date?"

"Yes. I just need someone to keep my mother—and the rest of my family—out of my hair, and the only way I'm going to do that is if I bring someone."

I rubbed my chin. "You want me to go with you as your fake date?"

"Fake date. Fake boyfriend."

"Oh, it's boyfriend now?"

"It's whatever I need it to be in order to have a peaceful weekend."

Scratching the back of my head, I said, "I don't know—"

"I'm willing to pay you."

"Hmm..." I shook my head. "Nah."

Panic took over her face. "That's it? Nah. You won't even think about it?"

I laughed. "I meant, nah to you paying me."

She gasped. "Does that mean you'll do it?"

"Yes, but instead of you paying me, I want a favor in return."

"What kind of favor?"

"I'm not sure yet. I'll let you know when I've decided." Another thought crossed my mind. "This arrangement, does it include sex?"

Her mouth dropped open. "What? *No.*"

I lifted a shoulder. "I was just checking. You know, because the dick costs extra. You'd owe me two favors instead of one."

When she stood there, unmoving, I walked over to her and pushed her chin up with a finger.

"Lighten up, Bree; it was a joke. If you're going to be uptight all weekend, then it really will cost you extra."

She scowled. "I'm not uptight," she huffed out.

"I guess we'll have to wait and see about that. What time do you need me on Saturday?"

She giggled awkwardly.

Not a good sign.

"Um, the thing is, it's actually from Thursday to Sunday, and it's out of town."

"Holy shit. Kind of left out some important details, huh?"

"Will you let me pay you now?" She clasped her hands together and begged, "Please don't say no."

"Fine. I'll need to move some stuff around for work, but I can manage it." I pointed my finger at her. "But know this: the favor I'm going to ask will be huge."

Chapter Four

BREE

"SO, WHY ME?" Zack asked me from the driver's seat of his SUV.

It was Thursday morning, and we were on our way to the lake resort for the wedding. It was about two hours north of Minneapolis-St. Paul, and he'd insisted on driving. I'd tried to tell him that it should be me to put wear and tear on my vehicle, but he'd said if we were really a couple, he'd be the one to drive. He'd also graciously told me I could chip in for gas.

Whatever. I hated driving anyway. I'd rather take a nap.

"Why you what?" I asked.

"Why did you ask me to go as your fake date to the wedding? We don't know each other that well."

"Honestly, because you were the first name that popped into my head when I lied to my mother about seeing someone."

He grinned. "And why did you think of me?" He wiggled his eyebrows.

"Get your mind out of the gutter. It was the morning after we ran into you at the restaurant. You were the last guy I saw." I shrugged. "And therefore, your name was the first that came to me."

I didn't mention it was also because my friends had already been talking about me bringing him to the wedding.

"But it's probably a good thing. Because before that, the last guy I saw was my coworker Jerry. He's around my mom's age, balding, with a potbelly, and he's married. My mother would never believe that I was dating him."

Zack laughed. "I agree. You're too sexy to date someone like that."

A tingle flared in my belly at his compliment, and I told my body to settle down. This was simply a platonic relationship.

"Thank you. And thank you for doing this. I'm actually surprised you said yes." I turned in my seat. "Why did you say yes?"

He shrugged. "Bored, I guess. I'm sick of doing the same ol' thing every weekend."

"And what is the same ol' thing?"

He shrugged again. "I don't know. Go on a date, fuck their brains out, and say good-bye before morning."

I blanched. "You know, you could go on a date with them more than once. Maybe break up the monotony a little."

He grimaced. "No, thank you. I am not into relationships." He leaned toward me. "Which is pretty much the definition of monotony."

"I think you're confusing monogamous with monotony."

"It's the same thing, babe."

"Okay then, how about you just go a weekend without getting laid?"

Zack gasped and put his hand over his groin. "Shh, you don't listen to her, big guy," he said, glancing down at his penis. "I would never do that to you."

I rolled my eyes and faced forward. "Tessa did say you were a manwhore."

"If you think that's supposed to be an insult, it's not working. And isn't *whore* derogatory? *Sex worker* is the correct terminology."

Eyeing him in surprise, I said, "Look at you. All woke and shit."

"Hey, just because I like sex doesn't mean I don't respect women. They go out with me, knowing full well what the rules are, and they always go home pleased." He smirked. "At least three times."

I snorted. *Yeah, right.*

Maybe some women, but there were plenty who could only come once and they were done. Like me. Not that I was going to say that. What if he took it as a challenge or something?

I shivered at the image of Zack between my legs as he smiled up at me.

Ugh. Why am I thinking about my friend's brother sexually?

No, no, no, no, no.

My core clenched, as if to say she didn't agree.

It was a good thing she didn't get a vote. She was the reason I'd ended up with my last boyfriend, and he had cheated on me.

"*Anyway,*" I said, "you're not a sex worker because you don't get paid. Manwhore will have to do. Unless you prefer man-slut? Player? Ladies' man? Playboy? Womanizer?" I chuckled at all the names I had come up with.

"Still not insulted, babe. Because you know what all of those titles have in common?"

"Egotistical men who can't keep it in their pants?"

He barked out a laugh and held up a finger. "One, I can keep it in my pants. I just choose not to if I don't have to. Two, I'm not egotistical."

I rested my elbow on the console in between our seats and stuck my chin in my hand. "Okay, hotshot, what's the answer then?"

"Good in bed."

"Yet you're not egotistical," I said dryly.

"Facts are facts, babe. My ego has nothing to do with it."

A thought occurred to me. I started giggling and couldn't stop.

Zack frowned. "What's so funny?"

"I just realized you're not going to have sex this weekend," I managed to tell him through my laughter.

He didn't seem to think it was funny. "I told you, I can go without sex. I'm not an addict or anything. Besides, you won't be the only woman there of banging age."

I bit my bottom lip as I grinned.

"What else did you leave out?" he asked with a sigh.

"It's just the wedding party and their guests who are going to be there this weekend. My cousin is marrying into money, and they booked the whole resort. If you have sex with someone else, it will make it back to me, and then we'll have to pretend fight or pretend break up. And if that happens, I'm taking back the favor I owe you."

"Well, shit."

"Yeah, so I guess we're going to see for sure if you can go without sex for a whole weekend."

"Oh, you'll see all right."

He took his eyes off the road to give me a once-over, and I resisted the urge to clamp my thighs together at the sight of the heat in his blue eyes.

"Unless you change your mind," he added.

I tilted my head. "About what?" I played dumb.

"About needing the dick."

"Oh, I won't change my mind."

Hot guys and their good-in-bed penises had already gotten me into too much trouble over the years. If I was ever going to date again, I was finding myself a eunuch.

I smiled sweetly at him. "Besides, if you gave me the dick, that means you would get the pussy. And if you had this pussy"—I waved a circle over my pelvis—"then I would no longer owe you any favors."

"Oh, who's egotistical now?"

"Facts are facts. *Babe.*"

Zack threw his head back and laughed. "I'll give you one thing, Bree—I'm definitely not bored."

Chapter Five

ZACK

WHEN WE GOT to the lake resort, we followed the signs to the private cabins, looking for cabin number four.

Out of nowhere, Bree put her hand on my arm and sat straight in her seat. "I forgot. The other reason I asked you was, when I brought up your name to my mom, she remembered meeting you one day when you were out with Tessa. Does that ring a bell at all? Otherwise, it's best you pretend to remember, so her feelings don't get hurt." She let go of me and reached for her phone. "Maybe I should find a picture of her to show you."

It would have been nice to have this information sooner than two minutes before we were going to meet up with her family, but since I was left with no choice, I did a quick mental recall.

Finally, I pictured my sister and me at Target, looking for a birthday present for our mom. An older woman had stopped Tessa to say hi, and my sister had introduced me.

"Is her name Diane?"

Bree looked up at me with astonishment. "Good memory. And close. It's Diana."

I smiled, satisfied with myself, but I was surprised that was Bree's mom. "I didn't realize that was your mother."

She had seemed closer to my grandparents' age than my parents'.

"She had me when she was thirty-eight. My dad never wanted kids, so I was a total *oops* baby. He passed away so you don't have to worry about meeting him."

I was thirty-one, which made Bree twenty-nine, making her mom close to seventy. My parents were in their mid-fifties. I'd been right about her mom being older.

"Sorry to hear that," I told her.

It was one thing to be an accident to people who wanted kids someday, but to find out you were never wanted had to be rough.

She shrugged. "It's fine. My mom always wanted children, but she constantly did everything my dad said, so she was secretly happy to have me. And my dad was...okay with it, I suppose."

I winced. A kid should have parents who were more than *okay* with them. It was a good thing the guy had already passed away because I had a feeling it would be hard for me to pretend to like the man.

I pulled up to the cabin, and before Bree and I could get our doors open, a swarm of women burst out of the front door.

Bree looked at me with a wary smile. "I apologize in advance for what is about to happen."

When I'd told Bree I agreed to do this out of boredom, I was being honest. I hadn't wanted to admit that doing the same thing every weekend with a different woman was becoming dull. I guessed a part of me thought that the next weekend would be more exciting. But when the next weekend came, it was the same as all the weekends before.

Maybe I was getting too old for the bachelor life. Who knew? But the thought of getting into a serious relationship made me jumpy. I didn't like that idea either. And sure, I could give up sex, but where was the fun in that?

But as the women all hugged Bree and turned to look at me, I had to wonder if boredom would be better than half a dozen set of female eyes on me. Each one studied me harder than the one before, it seemed.

Bree motioned me over to her side of the car with a head tilt. When I reached her, I stood close to her like a boyfriend would, but I didn't make any PDA moves since it was the first time I was meeting her family.

I wanted to say I knew which one was her mother, but all the older women looked the same. Maybe I should have had Bree show me a picture of her mom before we arrived.

Thankfully, my new fake girlfriend came to the rescue.

"Mom," she said to the woman right in front of us, "you remember Zack? Zack, this is my mom, Diana Keller."

I was ready to shake the lady's hand and maybe kiss her knuckles, but she caught me off guard when she pulled me into a bear hug.

My eyes flew up to Bree.

She shrugged, as if to say, *I already apologized before we got out of the vehicle.*

"Zack, I'm so happy you could come this weekend."

"Uh, thank you." I didn't know what else to do, so I patted Diana on the shoulder a few times and prayed she would let me go soon.

When she finally released me, Bree continued with introductions, "These are my aunts—Patrice, Jillian, Gina, and Maureen."

"How do you do, ladies?" I said with a grin, and they all smiled at me.

I didn't know why I'd been nervous for a minute there. Women of all ages loved me.

Bree turned to the younger women. "These are some of my cousins. Kylie is the youngest one. Then, there's Allie, and Tina is the bride."

"Hello," I said to her cousins.

Everyone stood there for a few more seconds before Bree started waving her arm. "Okay, you all came and met Zack. You can all stop staring at him now."

I didn't think they'd been staring at me, but they did disperse at Bree's command. Her mom, however, stuck around.

"How was the drive?"

"Good," I said.

"Where are we staying, Mom?"

"We're staying here, in cabin four," Diana said.

"But this is your cabin." I felt more than saw Bree tense. "Wait. What do you mean by *we*?"

"Oh, honey, I know you and Zack probably wanted a cabin all to yourselves, so you can...you know." Diana smiled knowingly.

Actually, we wanted our own cabin, so we wouldn't have to share beds. More like Bree did. I didn't mind if we had to share a bed, although waking up to her sweet curves every morning would give me raging wood.

"*Mom*," Bree chastised while I bit the inside of my cheek to keep from laughing.

Diana leaned forward. "I know kids these days don't wait for marriage to have relations. It's okay with me." She looked at me as she stood up straight. "I'm a cool, hip mom."

Bree groaned. "If that were true, you wouldn't need to announce that you were cool and hip." She spun around and went to the back of my SUV and opened the tailgate. "Can't you stay with one of your sisters?"

I followed her to help get our bags out of the back.

"Honey, the whole place is booked. I already checked because I thought maybe a room might be open, but I didn't have any luck. You only told me last week that you were bringing someone. But you don't have to worry. There are two bedrooms in the cabin. I'll keep my door closed and my earplugs in when I go to bed. I won't hear a thing." Diana winked at me.

Bree groaned, and when I looked at her face, I was pretty sure she was turning red.

Since there really wasn't anything we could do, I looked at her mom. "Thank you, Diana. Bree and I will be fine, staying with you. It's only for a few nights, right?"

She beamed at me and looked at her daughter. "Looks like you found yourself a gentleman, Bree." She looked down at our luggage. "I'll go open the door for you two. He's so much better than Rick."

Bree's mouth fell open.

"Who's Rick?" I asked.

"My ex, who she just asked about last Tuesday, wondering why I wasn't bringing him. My mother is unbelievable."

I swung my one and only bag on my shoulder and picked up one of the two she'd brought. Why she needed two pieces of luggage for one weekend, I would never understand.

"So, why is he your ex?"

"Because he cheated on me. Didn't stop my mom from asking me about him though." She sighed and headed for the door with me on her heels.

Chapter Six

BREE

I THREW my bag on the bed and began to hastily unpack it as I tried to fight off the tension headache that was building. I had been counting on the fact that once Zack and I were alone in our cabin, we wouldn't have to pretend, but now, we didn't even have that.

Zack brought the rest of our luggage in and closed the door behind him.

"Hey, it's not a big deal that we have to share a cabin with your mother. I think she likes me."

I snorted. "She loves you. But it still doesn't change the fact that we have to share a bed."

He shrugged. "It's just sleeping." A grin slowly spread across his lips. "Unless you think you can't keep your hands off of me."

His smile lit my panties on fire, but thankfully, I was upset enough to not let it show in the moment.

"I'm not that worried, trust me."

He frowned. "Then, what is it? Are you afraid I won't be able to keep my hands off of you?" He looked me up and down. "Because I'll be fine."

I knew I shouldn't say anything, but I opened my big mouth and said, "What's that supposed to mean?"

Was I not good-looking enough for him to sleep with? And why did I even care? This was an arrangement. That was it.

Zack held up his hands. "Nothing. It's just that you think I'm a manwhore or whatever. I can keep my hands to myself."

I sighed as my shoulders drooped. "We'll discuss it later."

I was hoping I'd be able to convince him to sleep on the floor since sleeping on the couch was out of the question. I didn't need my mother to think we'd had a fight or something. But we had hours to go before bed, so I would wait to ask him.

There was a small closet and dresser in the bedroom, so we unpacked some of our things. I watched Zack pull out a crisp white dress shirt and hang it in the closet. It looked like it had been kept nicely folded, but it was still full of wrinkles.

"Is that shirt for the wedding?" I asked.

"It is. Do you disapprove?"

"No, no, not at all. It's just—" I stopped when I got to the bottom of my suitcase and realized I had unpacked everything.

"It's just what?" Zack asked, but I wasn't listening.

"*No*," I cried out.

"What's wrong?"

"I left my dress and jewelry at home. I had it all set out on my dresser, ready to be packed..." Which was where it was probably still sitting.

"Is there anything else you brought that you can wear?"

"No. All I have are shorts, T-shirts, tank tops, and a bathing suit."

"I wouldn't mind if you wore the bathing suit to the wedding."

I jerked my head up and scowled at him.

Zack took a step back, holding his hands up. "Kidding."

"I'm not in the mood for jokes."

"Clearly."

I picked up my other bag, which had my cousin's wedding present in it. Even though I knew it was pointless, I began to search through it.

"Maybe you can borrow something from your mom?"

I snorted. "She's four inches shorter than me and at least two sizes smaller. Nothing she has will fit me even if I were desperate enough to borrow her clothes."

I reached the bottom of the second piece of luggage and heaved a giant sigh. Feeling hopeless, I collapsed onto the bed.

I knew it was just a wedding and that what I wore didn't matter *that* much. No one was hurt or dying, and my outfit wouldn't affect the wedding, but I was still frustrated and disappointed with myself.

Zack came over and pushed my bag out of the way, so he could sit. "How about this? We aren't that far from a town. Why don't we go tomorrow morning and find you something to wear?"

I picked at the string hanging out of my shorts. "I don't like you being nice to me."

He laughed. "Why not?"

"Because it's more fun to have someone to take my anger out on." I lifted my head and smiled at him.

"I suppose I could do something that would piss you off. Would that make you feel better?"

I tilted my head. "You'd do that for me?"

"Sure. You are my girlfriend, aren't you?"

I fell back onto the bed. "Pretend girlfriend. You don't have to go out of your way to do nice things for me when no one's around."

He stretched out onto an elbow. "It's not a big deal. But seriously, we can go into town, or if you want to take my vehicle, you can go by yourself. I'm fine either way."

I stared up into his handsome face. "That's very nice of you."

"I'm sure my sister left out the part about me being a nice guy when she helped you set this arrangement up." When he smiled, it almost looked like he had dimples under his short beard.

I couldn't decide if I would want to shave his face enough to find out because I also wondered what his facial hair would feel like against my skin.

Okay. It was time to get up and stop thinking about my *fake* boyfriend in a way I shouldn't be.

I practically jumped from the bed, leaving Zack to stare up at me in question.

"I think I'm going to check with some cousins and see if anyone has something I can borrow. And if not, then I'll go buy something tomorrow."

"Good thinking."

"Thanks. It sucks because I really like that dress." I lifted my arms in surrender. "But I suppose I have no choice." I turned around in a circle. "Now, where did I set my phone?"

Zack reached over onto the bed and picked up my mobile. "Here you go."

"Thanks." I hadn't even noticed that was where it had been lying.

"While you do that, I need to go outside and make a phone call."

"Okay," I said as I pulled up a new message thread and started adding every female cousin from seventeen to forty-seven.

Zack got up from the bed but stopped right in front of me. "Say, what are the plans today?"

"I think we're going down to the beach and grilling. And I'm sure someone brought their boat, so there might be tubing and skiing. Possibly a Jet Ski or two."

"Hmm..."

I tore my eyes from my phone. "What?"

"Oh, nothing. I was just thinking, I'll get to see you in your swimsuit."

I rolled my eyes and gave him a halfhearted shove.

He just laughed and spun around to keep himself from falling. "Don't worry, babe; you'll get to see me in my suit too." He held his arms out as he slowly walked backward toward the door, as if I was supposed to look at his body.

"Be careful."

He reached behind him and turned the knob. "Of what?"

"Oh, I just wouldn't want you to hit your massive ego on the way out."

Zack swung the door open and laughed as he walked out of the room.

Chapter Seven

ZACK

ONCE I WAS OUTSIDE, I looked around to make sure no one was around or at least within earshot.

I pulled up my sister's number and gave her a ring.

"Hey," Tessa answered. "How's it going?"

"Good. We just got here about twenty minutes ago. I met her mom and aunts. Everyone loves me already."

Tessa made a gagging noise, but I just laughed it off because that was what siblings did. We'd been giving each other crap our whole lives.

"Seriously though, Zack, thank you for helping Bree out like this. Her mom can be tenacious when it comes to Bree's love life, and I know you have relieved some of her stress."

"Until she opened her suitcase," I muttered.

"What?"

"I don't mind helping out a friend—or the friend of my

sister," I said. "But I was wondering if you had a way to get into Bree's house."

"I do," Tessa said cautiously. "But why do you want to know?"

"I know this is a big ask, which is why Bree probably wouldn't do it herself, but she forgot her wedding outfit on her dresser at home. Is there any way you could get it and bring it up here? I know it's about a two-hour drive, but I'd be willing to pay your gas. Or we could meet halfway."

My sister was silent on the other end.

"Shit, you're probably working."

My sister and Alexis—Tessa and Bree's friend—were working on opening up their own bakery business. They had set a plan about two years ago and were on track to open within the coming year, but when Alexis's husband had left her, he'd left her with some debt. So, she and Tessa had pushed their opening date out indefinitely.

I snapped my fingers. "I know. What if you overnight her clothes? It will be here by tomorrow, and since the wedding isn't until Saturday, that should be plenty of time. Hit me up with the postage amount, and I'll get you back." It was sure to be astronomical.

When my sister still didn't respond, I took a quick glance at my phone. It was still connected, and I had almost full bars.

"Tessa, are you still there?"

She cleared her throat. "Um, yeah. Yeah, I'm here."

"So, do you think you can do that for Bree?"

"Sure, sure. Let me see what I can do and get back to you."

I breathed a sigh of relief. "Thanks, sis. I won't say anything until you give me the all-clear that the package is on its way."

"I'll text you when I know something."

"Awesome. Thanks again."

"You're welcome. And, Zack?"

"Yeah?"

She paused. "Nothing. Never mind. I'll text you the deets when I have them."

This time, I didn't have to check my phone to see if my sister was gone. I knew she had already hung up.

I briefly wondered what she had been about to say to me, but I heard the creak of the cabin's screen door opening and watched as Bree stepped out.

I had ended the phone call just in time.

She looked at my phone and up to my eyes, and for some reason, I didn't want her to think I was talking to another woman.

"Tessa says hi."

When Bree smiled, I knew I had made the right call.

"I'll have to text her later. But right now, we're going to head down to the beach."

I did notice that she had a towel in her hands and the top of her swimsuit was tied behind her neck.

"Great. Give me a minute to get changed." I headed up the walk to the door.

"I also laid a towel out on the bed for you."

I spun around. "You mean, you're not carrying it for me?" I shook my head in mock disappointment. "Some girlfriend you are."

Her brow rose, and she put a hand on her hip. "This girlfriend is letting you see her in a bikini. You're coming out ahead in this deal."

I wiggled my eyebrows. "I can't wait." I opened the screen and remembered she had been texting with her cousins while I was on the phone with Tessa. "Hey, did anyone have extra clothes for you?"

"No," she said with a sigh. "I guess it's off to town tomorrow."

I nodded but smiled after I turned my back to her. I trusted my sister would come through, but I didn't want to get Bree's hopes up until I knew for sure.

I ducked into our bedroom and shucked off my shorts to slip on my swim trunks. As I came back out, I saw Diana in the kitchen.

"Are you coming down to the water with us?"

She looked up from the bowl she was stirring. "In a few minutes. I need to finish my pasta salad before I go down there."

I set down the towel that Bree had left on the bed for me. "Do you need help?"

Diana looked surprised. "Gosh, no. You and Bree go have fun. I'm almost done here."

"Are you sure?"

She smiled at me. "Yes. Now, go. And get my daughter to relax a little, will you? She's always uptight."

I felt bad for the two women. Diana obviously cared for and loved her daughter, but the pressure she put on Bree to get married stressed her daughter out.

I knew this because Bree had complained about it for about thirty minutes on our trip up to the resort.

"I'll try," I promised Diana.

Hopefully, my presence would help ease things between mother and daughter.

"Is your mom okay, cooking alone?" I asked Bree when I got outside.

"Yeah, she's fine. I already offered to help, and she pretty much kicked me out of the kitchen."

"Same."

Bree laughed.

"Okay, so she didn't kick me out, but she did tell me no."

She went from humor to a straight face. "Oh, you're serious."

I scoffed and walked past her toward the beach. "Of course I was serious. My mama didn't raise me to sit on my butt and have others do the work for me."

Bree ran after me, slowing to my pace when she reached me. "I should have realized. Whenever I was at your house, your mother always made me help your sister set the table or clean up the family room."

"And now, you know why I was never home. And why I moved out as soon as I got my diploma."

She laughed and gave me a hip check. "Your mom isn't that bad."

I smiled. "I know. I'm glad she gave me responsibilities. *Now*. But as a teenager, I had way more important things to do with my time."

"I get it. I didn't want to do anything like that in high school either."

I glanced over at Bree and was struck by how pretty she was. When the back of her hand brushed my knuckles, I took it in mine.

A startled expression crossed her face, and she looked at me.

"What?" I shrugged. "A boyfriend can hold his girl-friend's hand, can't he?"

"Good idea. It will look good when we show up with all my relatives there."

"Yeah, that's what I was thinking." Except that was just an excuse. I'd picked up her hand simply because I wanted to touch her.

What am I doing?

I knew I was playing with fire. She wasn't some woman I had picked up at a nightclub or bar or even on an app. She was my sister's friend, and I'd known her for years.

Yet I couldn't seem to help myself.

Chapter Eight

BREE

SO, it turned out that it wasn't Zack who wanted to see me in a swimsuit. Rather, it was me who wanted to see him in his.

He had on black trunks that hit him mid-thigh. His legs were long and tan with the perfect amount of leg hair. His shorts weren't tight, but they weren't loose, and every time he turned around, I wanted to squeeze his ass. And that was just the bottom half.

His chest was utterly lickable. His skin was smooth, his pecs defined, and his abs were of the washboard variety. He had a tattoo on the left side of his chest that read, *Rely on yourself, and you will not be disappointed.* And that was his only tattoo besides his left arm, covered from wrist to shoulder.

Had I mentioned that I was a slut for unilateral arm sleeves? I didn't know what it was about them, but they made me hot.

I hadn't planned on going in the water, but I might have to rethink that if I wasn't able to cool down.

I shouldn't—*couldn't*—be attracted to him for so many reasons. He was my friend's brother, I'd declared my body a no-man zone, and most importantly, he was a manwhore.

Zack and I spread our beach towels over some chairs lined on the beach, and I pulled out my sunblock.

I squeezed a large amount into one palm and started applying it to my bare skin. After I was finished, I handed the bottle out to Zack. "Do you want some?"

"Nah." He waved me off. "I don't burn."

The man had naturally bronze skin, but he could still get sun damage.

"You should apply some anyway."

"Don't need it." He jerked his head toward the back of my chair. "You need me to get your back for you?"

I looked at his sexy chest and long tan fingers. I wasn't sure what I would do if he touched me. "No, thanks. I'll be okay. I don't plan to lie on my stomach."

"Suit yourself, but you're probably going to burn."

"Says the guy who refuses to wear any at all."

He shrugged. "I'll be fine."

My cousin Sebastian made his way over to our chairs. "You two want to play Frisbee?"

If Sebastian and I weren't related, I would totally be attracted to him. He was muscular and built and even bigger than Zack. He had dark hair and dark eyes. No tattoos though, which was a shame. He'd look good with them. But alas, he was my cousin, and therefore, all my attraction was aimed at Zack.

I frowned. That wasn't right. I meant that I wasn't attracted to anyone.

I smiled. That was better.

"No, thanks," I said at the same time Zack jumped in and said, "Count me in."

Sebastian looked at me.

"Zack, my cousin Sebastian. Sebastian, Zack."

Sebastian smirked. "Ah, the new boyfriend."

He'd been teasing me since we were little, and since I was an only child, cousins were my substitute siblings.

"Just go and play," I commanded. "And, Zack?"

He looked down at me.

"If you happen to throw the Frisbee at Sebastian's head, I won't tell on you."

The two men started laughing and took off.

I was glad he'd already made friends with my family—my mother was going to love it—and now that I knew he wasn't paying attention to what I was doing, I couldn't keep my eyes off of him as he ran back and forth on the beach.

"Hey, Bree-Bree," a voice yelled as someone practically flew into the seat next to me.

I grinned at my cousin. "Hey, Lea-Lea."

Leah was only a year older than me, and ever since we had been little, we called each other by rhyming nicknames.

"Sorry I don't have an extra outfit for you. Besides my dress, I only brought casual vacation clothes."

"You and everyone else. But it's totally fine," I told her. "We're going shopping in the morning. I'm buying the first suitable thing I can find and getting out of there." I wanted to relax on the beach under the sun, not stand under fluorescent lights, looking at clothes.

"We, huh? How's the new boyfriend?" she said coyly to me. Both of us looked in Zack's direction. "He is hot."

"Thank you." I nodded my head toward Leah's husband, who was also playing Frisbee. "But it's not like Elliot isn't a looker himself." Sure, Zack was sexier, but I wasn't going to say that. "How is married life anyway? I feel like I haven't seen you in a long time."

"It's good. Can you believe it's already been a year?"

"Yes, I can because my mother reminds me every time one of her nieces has an anniversary."

Leah cracked up at this. "Oh, your mom will never change, will she?"

"I'm afraid not."

"I'm sorry you have to put up with her."

"No, you're not, or you wouldn't find it so funny."

Leah only laughed harder.

"I just want to know why my mother is the only one obsessed with marriage. Your mother never pressured you."

"Yes, she did," Leah protested. "But she wasn't as bad as Aunt Diana."

"How long did you and Elliot date?"

"Two years. And for one year and nine months, my mom hinted at marriage."

"So, it's a family trait, huh?"

"Must be."

"Remind me to not pass it on to my daughters."

Leah grinned. "Are you thinking about marriage already? From what my mom said, you and Zack only just started dating."

"Yeah, Bree, isn't it a little early to try and put a ring on it?" Zack said from behind me, and I stiffened as my face immediately heated.

"But—I wasn't—you misunder—it's not what you—" I sputtered and glared at him. "You know what? Maybe you should stop eavesdropping," I said defensively.

Zack chuckled.

"How did you end up behind me anyway?" I scowled. "The game is over there." I pointed in front of our chairs.

"You must have missed when the Frisbee flew over your head."

"So, Zack, would you let Bree put a ring on it?"

"Zack, this is my cousin Leah. Leah, this is my boyfriend, Zack."

Leah finger-waved, and I knew she was just having fun, but for some reason, it irritated me.

"And that tall, lanky guy you're playing with is Leah's husband of one year," I added.

"Elliot?" Zack said. "Congratulations. He seems like a nice guy."

Leah smiled. "He is."

Zack dropped down next to me and threw his arm over my shoulders. "As for this one, I think I'd let her marry me someday."

I turned my head toward him and tried not to look too hard at the glistening muscles that were only a few inches away. "You don't need to pretend like we're getting married," I said in a low voice. "Our relationship is new, remember?"

He pulled me close and put his mouth next to my ear. "Where's your sense of adventure? Let them think what they want."

"Yeah, until we break up and my mother is even more disappointed in me."

He loosened his hold. "Fair point," he said as I stared at his lips.

Looking around me, Zack said to Leah, "*Ixnay ethay arriagemay alktay*. Bree doesn't want her mom to be sad when she breaks my heart and leaves me."

"Ooh, and he speaks pig Latin. You'd better not break this one's heart, Bree."

"I won't." I looked at Zack.

If anything, he was the one who would break my heart.

Which was why he wasn't my real boyfriend in the first place. Because he didn't do relationships.

I pulled his arm from over my head. "You're gross and sweaty. You need to get away from me."

"Ouch. You wound me." Zack pretended to pull a knife out of his chest. "Here. I think you forgot this."

I playfully shoved him. "Get out of here."

He jumped to his feet. "See what I mean, Leah? Heartbreaker."

I snorted. "Yeah, right."

"Hey, man, are we playing or not?" Sebastian asked Zack as he sauntered up to our chairs. "Hey, Leah."

She waved back.

Zack made a circle with his finger. "Are you all cousins, or are any of you siblings?"

"Cousins," I answered. "My mom, Diana, is the oldest. Then, it's Sebastian's mom, Patrice. Next is aunt Gina; then Leah's mom, Maureen; and Jillian is the youngest."

"And the bride?"

"Tina's mom is Gina, the middle sister."

"I'm never going to be able to keep everyone straight," Zack said.

"Don't sweat it," Sebastian told him. "I can't keep track, and I'm a part of this family."

"Good to know." Zack flipped the Frisbee in his hand. "You ready to keep playing?"

"That's what I've been saying, haven't I?" Sebastian walked backward with his hands out.

Zack threw the Frisbee at him and looked at me. "See ya later, babe." He winked. "Just try to keep your tongue in your mouth when you watch me play this time."

Chapter Nine

BREE

Pru: I have a surprise for you!

WE WERE all stuffing our faces full of grilled hamburgers and hot dogs when the text from Pru came through.

Pru: Where are you?

I set my burger down on my plate to text her back.

Me: You know where I am. At the resort for my cousin's wedding. It's this weekend, remember?

Pru: Duh.

Pru: Never mind. Can you just come down to the main building?

I frowned. *What an odd request.*

Me: I'm confused.

Pru: LOL. Quit pretending like you don't
know. Now, get your butt moving, please.

I stood and slipped my phone in my pocket.

"Honey, where are you going?" my mom asked.

"Down to the main building."

Beside me, Zack froze mid-chew but only for a second. Then, he picked up his phone, as if searching for something, but he set it back down right away.

"Why?" Mom asked, and I turned my attention back to her.

"Because Pru told me to." I lifted my arms. "I don't know what's going on. I'll be right back."

Sebastian stood too. "Mind if I tag along? I wanted to check out the gym there."

"Not at all." I picked up my burger. "You're coming with me too."

"How's Indianapolis?" I asked Sebastian as we walked.

The beach was at the end of the resort, and the main building was at the entrance with all the private cabins in between.

"Eh, it's okay." Sebastian polished off his own burger and shoved his hands in the pockets of his swim trunks. "I'm actually thinking of moving back to Minnesota."

"Really? I would love to have you move back."

He was five years older than me, but Sebastian had been one of my closest cousins, growing up, since our moms were the two oldest sisters. It was harder to stay in touch though, living so many states apart.

Sebastian smiled at my excitement. "Yeah?"

"Yeah. What made you think about moving? Do you have a job lined up?" I took a bite of my burger and waited for him to answer.

"I don't know. Out of college, I liked the idea of moving far away, but now that I'm thirty-four, it's not as exciting. My dad's retired, and my mom will be in a year or so. I'm an uncle now. It would be nice to see my family more than twice a year."

"Speaking of being an uncle, where is your sister?"

"She and her family are coming tomorrow. My brother-in-law couldn't get today off work."

"What does your family say about you moving back?" I shoved the rest of my burger in my mouth.

"I haven't told them yet."

I was so surprised by this response that my food almost fell out of my mouth.

I quickly slapped my hand over my face, and the two of us started laughing.

After I managed to swallow, I smacked my cousin in the arm. "You should definitely move back, so we can have times like these."

"I'm working on it."

"Working on it? Is that why the fam doesn't know yet?"

He nodded and looked off into the distance. "I don't want to disappoint them if it doesn't work out."

"I understand. I won't say anything until you give me the all-clear."

We reached the main building, which had hotel rooms, a swimming pool, a recreation room, and a workout room, to name a few things.

Sebastian whistled. "Tina's fiancé must be loaded to rent out this entire place."

I laughed. "I was just thinking the same thing."

"Maybe we'll even get to meet the guy."

"Hey now, his money doesn't grow on trees. The man has to work for it, and that's why he's not here yet," I said with a smile.

"I see you got the same speech from Aunt Gina that I did."

"I think everyone in the family got that speech."

Sebastian opened the door for me.

"Thanks."

He followed in after me. "You're welcome. I'm going to look over the weight room. If you're ready to go back before me, don't feel like you have to wait."

As Sebastian took off in his search, I pulled my phone from my pocket, ready to call Pru.

"Hey, Bree, over here."

I looked in the direction where I thought my name had been called. It only took a few seconds, but then I spotted Pru hurrying toward me.

My mouth fell open. "What are you doing here?"

She frowned. "Didn't Zack tell you?"

"Zack didn't say anything." I held up my palm. "Wait. Zack knows you're here? Since when are you two friends?"

Pru hadn't said anything last week when Zack came up to our table, and irritation began to crawl at my insides. Zack was my boyfriend for the weekend, so why were he and Pru talking?

She wrinkled her nose. "We're not friends. Zack called Tessa and asked her to mail your clothes for the wedding up to the resort. But I was coming up north anyway, so I made a detour for you." She swung a plastic bag up and into my arms that I hadn't noticed she was carrying.

"What?" I quickly yanked the handles apart to look inside.

I was stunned.

Inside was my dress and the jewelry that had been sitting on my dresser. I lifted the dress to see that my sandals I had picked out were there too.

Rasing my head, I asked, "Who went to my house?"

"Tessa."

"I'm going to have to thank her. She even got my shoes that were sitting on the floor next to my dresser."

Pru cleared her throat, and I laughed as I looked at my friend.

"Thank you to you too." I pulled her in for a hug. "I really appreciate it. Now, I don't have to go shopping tomorrow morning. You are the best."

Rubbing my back, she said, "You're welcome. It gave me an excuse to check out this place anyway."

We separated, and I asked, "Since when were you interested?"

"Since you told me about it."

I couldn't help but smile. Pru was one of the top event and wedding planners at her job, and she was always on the lookout for new places.

"It's a little far from the Twin Cities, but it's great if you have people who want to get away. We've been down by the beach all afternoon."

"How are things going with Zack?"

"Good. My mother likes him already."

Just then, I saw Sebastian exit the hallway that he had previously gone down. He smiled when he saw me and started walking our way.

"I have to say, I wasn't on board with Paisley's idea at first, but it just might work out for you."

"Yep, she's smart. So, do you have to get back to work?" I asked, trying to get her off the subject of Zack being my fake date before Sebastian reached us.

She put a hand on her hip. "Are you trying to get rid of me?"

"No. It's just that I don't want anyone to overhear us talking about my *situation*."

Pru held her hands out and looked around. "Who's going to hear?" she said just as Sebastian came up behind her. "Nobody in here cares that you brought a fake date to your cousin's wedding."

Sebastian's eyebrows flew up in shock. "Holy shit. Zack isn't really your boyfriend?"

Chapter Ten

BREE

SHIT.

Now, my cousin knew my secret. Somehow, I'd have to convince him not to blab, but before I could think of how, Pru jumped and accidentally elbowed Sebastian in the stomach.

"What the hell?" She spun on her heel. "Who do you think...you are?"

What had started out as angry turned to bewilderment, and I studied my friend. I wasn't sure she was okay.

Meanwhile, my cousin was rubbing his stomach and scowling at her. "There's no need to resort to violence."

Grabbing Pru's arm, I pulled her back toward me.

"Pru, this is my cousin Sebastian. Do you remember him from when we were little?"

Pru gasped and narrowed her eyes. She was back to anger. "*Yes.* He threw a frog at us when we were playing in your backyard."

I laughed. "I forgot about that."

Sebastian smirked and shoved his hands in his pockets. "You two wouldn't leave me alone."

"We were *five*," Pru explained.

"And I was probably around ten. I didn't want to play with annoying girlie babies."

"Thankfully, we've grown up," I interceded. "Sebastian doesn't throw frogs on others anymore. And, Pru, we probably were annoying, but I don't think we are anymore."

Sebastian grinned at me. "Well, I know one of you isn't."

Pru tensed up.

"Who's being annoying now? Knock it off, Sebastian." I tugged on Pru's arm. "He's just trying to get a rise out of you. Stop taking the bait," I said with a chuckle.

"He's being mean," she mumbled.

"Says the woman who elbowed me in the solar plexus."

"Sebastian, why don't you wait for me outside while I say good-bye to Pru?"

"Sure."

We watched my cousin walk out the door, and as soon as it closed behind him, Pru said, "What an asshole."

"He's not that bad, which is good because now, I have to go and beg him not to tell anyone about Zack."

She winced. "I'm sorry. I didn't realize that you had come to the building with someone else."

I sighed. "I told you the bride's fiancé rented the whole place for the weekend. I know it's only Thursday, but there's a good chance I'll know anyone walking around."

"You're right. I'm sorry. Again." She picked up my free hand and clutched it to her chest. "Don't hate me."

I rolled my eyes. "I could never hate you. I'm not even mad at you because I know it was an accident. But I should go before Sebastian gets bored and heads back to our families without me." I jiggled the plastic bag I was holding. "Thank you again for bringing this to me. I really do appreciate it."

"You're welcome." Pulling me in for a hug, she said, "Good luck with your dick of a cousin. I hope he doesn't say anything to anyone."

"He's good. I'm sure he won't...as long as I swear him to secrecy."

Pru let me go and backed away. "I'm parked on the other side. Let's talk later, okay?"

"Okay. I'll text you."

Waving good-bye, she headed for the far entrance while I went to the other.

When I walked outside, Sebastian turned around. "So, that's your friend Pru, huh?"

I eyed him. Could he be interested in my friend? Should I warn him that she'd sworn off men, like me? I couldn't tell for sure if he liked her or if he was just trying to picture the little girl from when we had been kids. And since he lived far away from us, there was no point in telling him that he didn't have a chance with her.

"Yeah. Do you remember the frog incident? Because I don't."

"Kind of. But I was older than you. I'm more surprised she remembered."

"She has a way better memory than me. Don't cross her. She'll hold it against you until you die."

"Apparently," he said dryly.

"So, we should probably talk about what you heard in there," I said as we started walking back to the beach.

"Yeah, what is up with that?"

I didn't expect Sebastian to understand because he was a guy, but I was going to have to try to explain if I wanted him to keep my secret.

"Zack is the brother of Tessa, my and Pru's friend. You might remember her?"

"Maybe. Not sure."

"Anyway, he's doing me a favor. And the reason he's doing me a favor is because of my mother. She won't leave me alone about getting married. And I am"—I threw my fists up and groaned—"so sick of it."

"I don't get it."

I scoffed at him. "Of course you don't. You're in your mid-thirties, and no one harasses you constantly about when *you're* going to get married."

He held up a finger. "Now, now. My mother and sister ask about my love life."

"But do they hound you about marriage?"

"No," he admitted sheepishly.

"Do you know that my mom wanted me to stay with my last boyfriend even though he'd cheated on me?"

Sebastian looked taken aback. "That's fucked up."

"*Thank you.* At least someone in this family agrees." I sighed. "I blame my father. He was a serial cheater, so my mom thinks it's normal."

"Don't say anything, but I think Grandpa wasn't faithful to Grandma either."

My jaw dropped. "That explains so much." I hit my cousin in the arm. "How do you know that?"

He grinned. "My mom and dad had too much tequila one night. I honestly doubt they even remember telling my sister and me." He chuckled. "That's also when I found out my mother had threatened to cut my dad's balls off if he ever did the same to her."

I laughed at the image. My aunt was little but feisty.

"I wish my mom were more like yours."

"I understand. But your mom is the oldest. She probably sacrificed some things to keep her younger sisters from knowing because I don't think my mom found out until high school."

A strange sense of pride filled me at the idea of my mother protecting her sisters, and it made me a little less annoyed with her. But it was still hard for me to give her my complete respect when she didn't break the cycle. My grandma had had five kids in the '40s and '50s. She'd had to stay. But my mother had been childless for many years. There had been nothing stopping her from leaving my father. But Sebastian was right. It was sad.

I kicked a rock in front of me. "I kind of wish Grandma were still around. I would go and give that woman a medal for putting up with that shit while raising so many kids."

"Yeah. Me too. Maybe when I move back, you and I can take flowers to her grave."

"I like that idea." I smiled slyly. "And we'll take Grandpa a lump of coal for being a shitty husband."

Sebastian barked out a laugh. "Count me in."

We were almost to cabin number four.

"Hey, I need to drop off these clothes real quick."

"Wait," Sebastian said before I could open the door, and I walked back to him.

"Why did you have to find a fake date for this weekend? You're gorgeous. There must have been guys lining up to come to this thing with you."

"Oh, I'm not dating anymore."

His eyes flew open. "Why not?"

"Because men suck." I put my hand on his arm and smiled sweetly. "Oh, and if you tell anyone about my situation, I'm going to let everyone and their dog know that you are moving back to Minnesota. I'm not sure who will get more questions. You or me."

"You are evil."

I shrugged. "All's fair in love and war...and family."

Chapter Eleven

ZACK

I DIDN'T REALIZE how much I had been waiting for Bree to come back until I saw her walking toward the beach.

When she had taken off because her friend Pru had shown up, I had checked my phone repeatedly to see if my sister had sent her. But there were no messages from Tessa, and she hadn't replied to the last few I had sent her.

Bree and Sebastian exchanged looks right before they reached the group and went off in different directions. She turned her gaze toward the crowd and searched. When her eyes landed on me, she headed straight toward me.

She barely paused when she reached me. Then, she clasped my hand and pulled me away from everyone. "I need to talk to you."

Her mother and other family members looked our way, so I shrugged with a smile to let them know everything was okay.

Bree had sounded serious, but I didn't want them to think there was a problem between us.

We strolled down the beach, hand in hand, and I waited patiently for Bree to tell me what was on her mind.

After a few seconds, she spit out, "Sebastian knows you're not really my boyfriend."

That wasn't what I had been expecting, and it took me a second for my brain to process.

"Oh. Oh shit."

She waved away my concern. "It'll be fine. He's not going to tell anyone. But I wanted you to know that he's aware." She chewed on her bottom lip. "Knowing him, he'll give the two of us crap about it, but he won't tell anyone."

"Are you sure?"

"Yeah, I trust him." She grinned. "Plus, I have a little secret of his that I blackmailed him with. Our secret is juicier, but he doesn't want anyone to know his."

"Do I get to know this secret, so I can also threaten him?" I asked.

"Just that he's planning on moving back to Minnesota."

I raised my brow. "That's it? That's the secret?"

Bree chuckled. "Trust me, he doesn't want everyone to know because they will ask a million and one questions. Constantly."

"Ah. I get it now."

"Families. They want to get in everyone's business."

"So, how did he find out?" I frowned. "Did he guess? Do we need to up our boyfriend-girlfriend game?"

"No. Pru was blabbing about you being my fake date,

and Sebastian came up behind her and overheard. She hadn't known he was behind her."

"That sucks."

"Yeah. It is what it is, I guess." She slowed our pace and brought us to a stop. "There's something else I wanted to ask you about."

"Okay."

When I turned to face her, a lock of hair had escaped her ponytail. I brushed it off her cheek and settled it behind her ear. "What's up?"

She smiled shyly. "Did you really ask your sister to get my wedding clothes to me?"

I beamed. "You got them?"

"Yes. That's why Pru was here. She said you asked Tessa to get them up here, but she was coming north anyway, so she brought them instead."

"Technically, as we left it, I asked her to send them overnight through the post office or UPS or something. That was nice of Pru to hand-deliver them."

"It was."

I pulled out my phone. "I'll have to thank her."

Bree pushed my hand down. "I already thanked her for the both of us."

"Oh." It was kind of odd she didn't want me to text Pru, but maybe she thought I had gone out of my way to do enough. "Okay."

"But I do need to tell your sister thank you."

"If you can get ahold of her. She isn't answering any of my messages."

"Regardless, thank you for doing that for me. That was really...sweet of you."

I cringed. "No, I'm not sweet." Chicks didn't want to sleep with "sweet" guys. "Doing someone a favor is not sweet. You're going to ruin my rep."

"So, you're saying I owe you another favor?"

"Well, no."

She grinned. "Then, it was sweet." She tugged on my arm—I'd almost forgotten we were still holding hands—and pulled me back toward her family. "We'd better get back."

I slowed down, digging in my heels. "I'll go back as long as you take back that awful thing you said about me."

Yanking harder on my hand, she said, "Fine. I take it back. You're not sweet."

I immediately stopped resisting. "Thank you."

Bree smiled slyly over her shoulder. "I'm just going to tell everyone what a nice guy you are instead." She let go of my hand and sprinted away.

"What are you thinking? That's even worse," I yelled as I ran after her.

I caught up to her in about ten feet. Flipping her around, I leaned over and lifted her over my shoulder.

"Put me down, Zack."

"No way. Haven't you ever heard, nice guys finish last? I refuse to finish last."

"I thought finishing last would be something guys like you would brag about."

It took me a second to realize she was referring to finishing last in the bedroom.

I slapped her ass, and she yelped. "You know what I mean."

Her family stared at us as we neared. Some were laughing, and others looked on with speculation.

"Put me down, you big jerk."

"Finally. Was that so hard?" I set her on her feet, holding on to her hand to make sure she didn't fall.

"What's going on?" Diana asked.

Bree smiled again. The same one she'd just given me before she ran off. "Nothing much. Just that Zack here found a way to get my wedding outfit to me."

Diana put her hand on her chest. "Oh my, what a sweet man."

Bree stuck her tongue out at me. "Told you, you're sweet."

Leah, her cousin, lifted her hard lemonade toward the back of the crowd. "What a man. I think that deserves a BJ as a thank-you."

Bree stiffened. "Oh my God, someone needs to take away her alcohol," she said in a low voice.

Sebastian, who was standing next to Leah, also added his two cents. "I agree. She owes you, Zack." He winked at me and stuck his tongue in his cheek while shoving his fist toward his mouth.

Diana looked at me in confusion. "Are you a big Burger King fan, Zack?"

I burst out laughing.

"Mom, that's BK."

"Oh." Diana looked down at the sand, lost in thought, as if the wheels were still turning in her head.

I threw my arm around Bree and put my mouth near her ear. "Remember how I said it wasn't a favor? I change my mind. A BJ sounds really good right about now."

"My blow-job skills are worth way more."

I can't wait to find out.

Wait. No. Bad Zack.

I was not supposed to be having thoughts like that.

Shit.

This fake relationship with Bree was about to get me in a ton of *real* trouble.

Chapter Twelve

BREE

"WE ARE NOT SLEEPING in the same bed." I stomped my foot a little too loudly on the floor of our bedroom.

It was late, and we'd finally come back to our cabin to sleep. My mom had slipped away from the beach about an hour earlier than us and was already in bed. I needed to be careful not to wake her to find us fighting.

But it was hard not to freak out.

Zack had hopped in the shower the second we got back and climbed into bed without any hesitation. He hadn't even asked me if I was okay with the situation.

He pointed to the door. "You're more than welcome to sleep on the couch."

"Yeah, and have my mother ask if we had a fight? I don't think so."

He leaned over the bed and looked down. "There's always the floor," he said with a smile.

I pouted like a stubborn child. "I thought you would be the one to sleep on the floor."

He snorted. "I'm thirty-one. I can't sleep on a hard-wood floor. If I were twenty-one and sloshed, maybe, but not nowadays, especially with only a few beers in my system. Our deal did not include crappy sleep and being sore the next day." He held out his hand. "But you're more than welcome."

He had a point. He was doing me a favor, and it wasn't fair for him to sleep on a floor that didn't even have a rug. But that didn't mean I was happy about it.

I huffed out a breath and picked up my pajamas from my suitcase. "I'm going to shower," I said and trudged to the one and only bathroom in the hall.

I stripped off the sweatshirt and shorts I had put on after the sun went down and removed the swimsuit I still had on underneath my clothes.

As I pulled off my top, I noticed that it hurt my back a little, so I inspected it to see if I had missed the plastic part from a tag. I had washed my suit after purchasing it, but this was the first time I had worn it.

Nothing was poking out anywhere, so I hung it up on the towel rack and got in the shower. I left my hair up, only washing my body to get the sunblock and sand off my skin. I noticed the hot water stung my back a little, but I brushed it off as nothing.

It wasn't until I was out of the shower, brushing my hair, that I realized I had gotten a sunburn. My hand slipped off my hair, the brush scraping my back, and I howled in pain.

I turned around to look and saw I was pink from shoulders to waist.

"*Shit.*"

There was a knock on the door, and I jumped.

"Are you okay in there?" Zack asked.

"Yes, I'm fine," I quickly answered.

I heard his footsteps disappear, and it occurred to me that there was no way I was going to get lotion or aloe on my back by myself. And I needed to do something, so I wouldn't be miserable tomorrow.

This wasn't the first time I had gotten sunburned, and it wouldn't be the last. I had actually packed aloe in my bag, knowing there was a chance I would probably need it.

I put on my pajama shorts and held my shirt to my chest as I exited the bathroom.

Lightly, I knocked on my mom's door and peeked in. She was sound asleep. I waited a second to see if she would rouse, but she was completely out.

With my head held high, I headed to my shared bedroom. Zack was on his phone but looked up when I entered.

He didn't say anything, but his eyebrow went up when he saw I wasn't wearing my shirt.

"I need a favor. I wouldn't ask you if I had anyone else, but my mom is asleep."

He set his phone down. "What do you need?"

I went to my suitcase, scrounged around in it for a few seconds, and lifted out my bottle of aloe with lidocaine. I held it out to him. "I need you to put this on my back. Please."

Zack bit his lip, like he was trying not to laugh, as he got up and walked around to my side of the bed.

"What's so funny?" I challenged even though I'd already anticipated what he was going to say.

"Oh, nothing."

I shoved the aloe at him. "Liar. Spit it out."

He lifted his chin. "Turn around."

I did as I had been told, pushing my hair over one shoulder to get it out of the way.

"I might find it comical that you wouldn't put on sunblock at the beach. I believe you told me you didn't plan to lie on your stomach, but I guess you forgot about all the walking around you would be doing."

Not to mention, I had sat, facing away from the sun, when we ate, so it wouldn't be in my eyes. I had been so adamant on not letting Zack touch me that I had foolishly gotten burned.

In hindsight, I should have let him put sunblock on me in public because, now, he had to rub something all over me in the privacy of the bedroom we were sharing.

"Are you ready?" he asked me.

I nodded. "Yes."

"Let me know if I hurt you."

"Okay."

I heard the bottle being squeezed and set on the

dresser, and a few seconds later, the soothing coolness of the aloe hit my skin.

I must have made a noise because Zack stopped moving his hands.

"I'm fine. The cold surprised me. But it feels good," I reassured him.

He gently covered my back with the aloe, taking his time to spread it everywhere.

At one point, I closed my eyes, enjoying the feel of his palms running over me. I was tired, and I almost went into a dreamlike trance, where I imagined his touch moving from my back to my arms to my front. He would pull me back against—

"All done. I'm going to wash my hands." Zack stepped back and left the room.

As soon as I was alone, I hastily put on my pajama top and tried to cool my heated cheeks. I couldn't believe I had been fantasizing about the man.

I took several deep breaths in and out and counted to ten. And when that didn't quite work, I pictured my ex-boyfriend in my head.

That did the trick.

The water turned off in the bathroom, and I was pulling back the covers on my side of the bed when he came back in.

"So, you resigned yourself to sharing a bed with disgusting ol' me?" Zack joked, pushing thoughts of Rick from my mind.

I sat. "You're not disgusting, and you know it."

It was more the opposite. I didn't want to share a bed with *sexy* ol' Zack.

"Besides, there is no way I'm sleeping on the floor. Especially now. Too painful." I had considered sleeping on the floor but not with my sunburn. My back hurt, just thinking about it. "But I was thinking of making a few rules."

He crossed his arms over his chest and grinned. "Let me have them."

"We both stay on our own sides of the bed."

"Okay."

"Which means no wandering hands or feet."

He rolled his eyes. "I'm not five. I understand keeping my hands and feet to myself."

"And how many pillows do you need to sleep with?" I asked.

His brow lifted. "One."

I smiled. "Good." I swung around. "We have four pillows, so we can put two between us."

I flipped back the covers and placed the extra two in the middle of the bed. It was a queen-size mattress, so we both still had plenty of room to sleep.

Zack just shook his head at me as he walked around to his side. "I've never had a woman go to so much trouble not to touch me."

"There's a first time for everything."

"I guess so." He reached behind him and pulled off his shirt.

Now, I had seen the guy shirtless all day, but for some

reason, seeing his bare, muscular chest in the dim light of the bedroom we were alone in was much different.

I was tempted to tell him to put his tee back on, but I didn't want him to think I was affected by him. I turned off the lamp next to my bed and slid under the covers. I gently patted the pillows next to me for reassurance. They were my security blanket tonight.

Zack flicked the switch on his own light, and the bed dipped as he got in.

I closed my eyes, surprised that sleep was already starting to claim me.

"I have a rule too."

My lids flew open, and my heart sped up.

"What rule could you possibly have?" I managed to put a little annoyance in my voice.

"If you come to my side of the bed, all bets are off."

Yeah, right. That's never going to happen.

Chapter Thirteen

BREE

IT HAPPENED.

By morning, I was in the middle of the bed and then some with one barrier pillow on my side and the other who knew where.

But Zack was still on his half.

I was lying on my stomach, halfway across his chest, with his hand on my ass, and it was all my fault.

And when I said, on my ass, I meant, on my ass. There was a *hand up my shorts and on my bare butt* situation going on.

Sometime during the night, I had crossed the threshold and plastered my body to his.

Shit, shit, shit. And now, I somehow had to extract myself from him without waking him up.

I had no idea where to start.

But after some quick, strategic planning in my head, I slowly came up with a way to pull his arm from my behind and roll away in a couple of swift moves, all while holding my breath.

By the time I made it to my side of the bed, my heart was racing, and I felt like I had run a marathon. It would be a good bet that my blood pressure was through the roof.

I only gave myself about thirty seconds for my adrenaline level to lower before I got up and put the pillows back to where they had been when we went to sleep. I found the second one on the floor.

What did I do in my sleep?

Hopefully, snuggling up to Zack was the worst thing, and I hadn't tried to feel him up or anything.

I shivered at the thought and slowly turned on my heel, half-expecting him to be watching me.

But he was still asleep, his breathing deep and even, and I decided I was in the clear.

I watched him for a few minutes, admiring his chiseled face and amazing pecs. I wasn't sure if I would be prepared to find out what he'd meant by "all bets are off" if I went to his side of the bed. And thankfully, now, I didn't have to.

———

ZACK

I waited patiently for Bree to go through her luggage, grab whatever she needed, and leave the room before I reached down and adjusted my aching hard-on.

I had woken up about twenty minutes before Bree,

shocked as hell when I found her sleeping on top of me with my hand on her ass.

I had warned her about coming over to my half of the mattress, but I had only been messing with her. Did it mean I would turn her down if she got naked and spread her legs for me? *Hell no*. I was a male with a healthy appetite for sex after all.

But she had made her way over to me in her sleep, and it just wasn't the same if she didn't want to be with me.

So, I had lain there and pretended to be sleeping, my only sin not taking my hand off her delicious butt.

Waiting for her to try to get herself out of my embrace had been worth it even if I had to play dead.

I threw the covers off the bed and got up when Bree walked back in, dressed for the day.

"Oh, you're awake."

I lifted my arms over my head and arched my back as I stretched. "Yeah." I stood straight, feeling better now that some of the kinks were out. "What's on the agenda today?"

My luggage was next to me, and I reached in for the first shirt and shorts I could find when I realized that Bree hadn't answered me.

I looked over at her to find her staring at me, zoned out with her eyes wide.

"Bree."

"Huh?" She shook her head, as if shaking off her trance. "What did you say?"

I pulled my shirt over my head. "I asked, what's on the agenda today?"

When my head popped through the neck of my shirt, I caught Bree staring at my junk.

Naughty girl.

I snapped my fingers in front of my crotch and said, "My eyes are up here," before pointing at my face.

Her cheeks turned red as she lifted her chin. "Brunch at the resort's restaurant and then a combined bachelor-bachelorette party."

I turned my back to her. "How does that work?" I asked as I pushed my sleep shorts off my hips and put on my boxer briefs and bottoms for the day.

And I realized that once again, Bree hadn't answered me.

I spun around to find myself alone in the bedroom, so I went to find her.

She was in the kitchen with her mom, drinking coffee and not looking at me.

"Coffee?" Diana asked as I went to stand beside Bree.

"Please. Bree said there is brunch. What time is that?" I normally ate right away when I got up, and I didn't know how long I would sit around and wait.

"Nine thirty," Diana said as she walked to the corner of the kitchen where the coffeemaker was.

"Nine thirty?" I said, horrified. "It's only a little after eight."

I heard Diana chuckle, but Bree continued to ignore me as she sipped from her cup.

I leaned close. "Everything okay?"

"You stripped right in front of me," she hissed.

I frowned. "It was just my ass. And I had a shirt on. I wasn't completely naked," I said in a low voice.

"Still, you need to warn a lady first."

"I think you forgot that we're supposed to be dating. You're supposed to have seen a lot more than my naked ass. I could have faced you, and then you would have seen my di—"

"*Just don't do it again.*"

I backed away. "Sheesh. I never took you for a prude," I said under my breath.

She shot me a dirty look, and I rolled my eyes.

Now, she looks at me.

Diana carefully turned around and carried my coffee to me. "Do you want any creamer or sugar?"

I smiled at her. "Thank you. And no, I'm fine."

Bree's mom looked at her and me and furrowed her brow. "Is everything okay?"

"Just a misunderstanding, is all," my fake girlfriend said.

I snorted, and she gave me another look.

"Well, you'd better make up if you want to win today."

"Win what?" Bree and I both asked at the same time.

Diana's eyes brightened at our collective question. "It's supposed to be a surprise, but at the party this afternoon, there are going to be couples games, and the more you win or the better you score..." She waved her hand in front of her, as if she couldn't quite remember the rules. "Basically, you get a prize at the end." She took a drink of her coffee. "Rumor has it, it's going to be something good."

"What if you're not in a couple?" Bree asked.

She didn't sound happy, and I assumed she didn't like the idea of only people in relationships being able to participate. I understood the feeling. Us single people wanted to participate too.

"It doesn't have to be a romantic couple," Diana explained. "Just two people. There's talk of a three-legged race and stuff like that."

"Hmm..." Bree said. "How about you and I be a couple, Mom? We haven't spent enough time together."

I scoffed. *Is she really that pissed that I took my shorts off in front of her?*

"Oh, no, I won't be there. Your aunts and I are going into town for some shopping." She smiled at the two of us. "This is for you young kids. You're supposed to have fun without the parents around. It is a bachelor and bachelorette party. Nobody invites their parents to those." Diana laughed like we were silly for even thinking she'd be there.

I grinned and threw my arm around Bree. "Looks like you're stuck with me, babe."

She met my eyes. "Then, you'd better be prepared to win, *babe*." Her jaw clenched. "Because I don't like to lose."

No problem there. She was about to learn that when I played, I played to win.

Chapter Fourteen

BREE

"ATTENTION, EVERYONE," my cousin Tina said as she clapped her hands.

Brunch had ended some time ago, and Zack and I had made our way from the banquet hall over to a field that, apparently, the bride and groom had reserved for their party. There were already people there. Many were members of my family, but there were others I didn't recognize. And the field had various areas set up, including a table behind the bride and groom.

Tina's fiancé, Nelson, who had arrived that morning, leaned over and whispered in her ear.

Tina giggled, putting her hand on his arm and leaning in close.

I was happy for Tina. She and Nelson seemed to really like each other as well as be in love.

"Damn, how many acres is this place?" Zack asked in my ear.

I shrugged as a way of answering him.

I knew I was being unreasonable, but after waking up in his arms and then seeing him looking so sexy this morning, I was trying to keep my distance. I was done with men, and I had best remember that.

But staying away from him was absolutely ridiculous if I wanted my family to think we were dating.

I mentally rolled my eyes at myself. I had asked Zack to be my fake date for this wedding, and now, I was treating him like I was mad at him. We'd had brunch with Leah and Elliot, Sebastian, and a few of my other cousins, so no one had noticed I wasn't speaking to Zack because plenty of others were talking. But people were going to suspect something was amiss if I didn't get over myself.

I needed to face the facts. Zack was sexy, even fresh out of bed and not even trying, and I had better get used to it. It was only a couple more days, and then I could go back to seeing him sporadically, like I had before this stupid weekend.

In an effort to be nicer, I met his eyes. "I checked out the website before we came, but I don't think it said how much land the resort is on."

He smiled. "So, done ignoring me, are you?"

"I wasn't ignoring you," I lied.

"Hey, Bree and Zack."

We turned to see Leah and Elliot approaching.

"Hey," I said. "Have you heard any rumors about what is happening here?"

"Nothing," Leah said. "You?"

"Same." My competitive nature was stronger than my love for my cousin.

Zack snickered, and I elbowed him in the gut.

Nelson put his hands in the air. "It's been decided."

"What's been decided?" someone in the crowd yelled.

Nelson shot the person a look. "If you'd let me finish, you would find out."

"Sorry," the person yelled, not sounding the least bit apologetic.

"Here's what we're going to do," Nelson said. "We're going to break up into couples, and whichever couple wins the most races will get"—Tina reached behind her and swung her arm around to show us—"this trophy."

There were a couple grumbles in the crowd, but I was polite and clapped.

Nelson and Tina grinned at each other.

"And how does two hundred bucks sound?" Nelson asked.

That got him a bunch of cheers.

"What if we're not in a relationship or our significant other couldn't make it?" someone toward the front asked.

"You can pair up with anyone you want," Tina clarified. "A friend. A family member. We just want everyone to have fun. But if you still don't have someone, you can help us judge. But you have to promise to be fair because Nelson and I decided on something else." She grinned and wiggled her eyebrows.

"We're going to pit my guests," Nelson said, "against my beautiful bride's side. Whatever side has the most winners will get free drinks tomorrow night at the wedding reception."

"You're having an open bar," came from the crowd.

I was pretty sure that was the voice of the same guy who had heckled Nelson, and I had to chuckle.

"Oh, that's right," Nelson said in a way that showed he hadn't forgotten. "I guess that means we're giving the winners free drinks at tonight's rehearsal dinner."

There were claps and cheers and even a whistle or two.

"All right, let's start by breaking up into two groups. My family and friends on my left and Nelson's on my right."

Leah, Elliot, Zack, and I moved over to the left. After we split up, it seemed like the sides were pretty even, except there was a couple standing in the middle.

"We can't decide whose side to be on," the woman said. "You're my best friend, and he's Nelson's." She pointed to the man standing next to her.

"How would you like to help us judge?" Tina offered.

"Will we still get to drink for free tonight?"

Nelson laughed. "Sure."

"We have one other person who offered to help us judge," Tina said. "Sebastian?"

I hadn't even realized he had come. I thought he would have skipped out since he was single, but he came out of nowhere and joined Tina and Nelson.

"We'd like you to split up into couple teams now. If there is anyone else who doesn't have a partner, let us know." Tina arched up on her tiptoes and started counting under her breath as Zack and I stepped away from everyone else to show we were together. "My side has eight couples."

"Mine has seven," Nelson said.

Two women I didn't know very well, except for the fact that they were friends with Tina, raised their hands. "We could help judge," one of them said.

"Perfect," Tina said. "Come on up. That makes seven judges, including Nelson and me. I think we're good, don't you?"

Nelson nodded and pointed off to the left behind us. "Before we get started on the first game, we have refreshments. And by refreshments, I mean, we have alcohol, pop, and water. If you want something, go now because the first game we're going to play is a three-legged race. You'll see there is a line at the top of all your glasses. Not only are you going to be tied to each other, but you also have to hold a drink filled to the line and not spill any. Every time you spill, you get five seconds knocked off your time. When you get to the end, you have to drink everything in your glass and turn around and go back the other way."

I liked that they had added a spin on the three-legged race. And it gave me an idea on how we could win.

I grinned at Zack. "So, what happens if we *accidentally* spill all the contents right away?" I wiggled my eyebrows. "Only five seconds are cut off, but we can make it up when we pick up speed."

"That's cheating," he said and headed for the table.

I took off after him. "No, it's called playing the game."

"It's cheating," he said over his shoulder. "And we're not doing it."

"You mean, you're not doing it. I can do whatever I want," I said only to myself as we reached the refreshments.

Zack leaned over. "It's not going to help you when I still can't go fast."

I curled my lip at him. "You're no fun."

"I'm loads of fun. You just wait. We're going to win this without cheating."

We waited our turn without another word to each other. I had planned to get water, but when Zack chose beer, I figured I might as well too. The whole thing would be more fun with a little alcohol.

"All right," Nelson said. "Bride's side goes first. We set up a little area for relay races. It only has five lanes, so to have all fourteen couples race, we'll have to run three heats."

"Let's get up there right away," Zack said, grabbing my hand as he started walking. "Let's get it over with, so we don't let everyone else's time get in our heads."

"I think you're taking this way too seriously for someone not willing to cheat," I said as he dragged me behind him. "Be careful. You're going to make me spill, and we're not even there yet."

Zack and I made it up as the last couple of the first heat. Sebastian came over to us. He had a piece of rope in his hand, and he was pretending to snap it with a goofy smile on his face.

"Zack, are you ready to tie my cousin up?"

"You're not funny, Sebastian," I told him with a chuckle.

"Then, why are you laughing?"

He had me there.

Sebastian pushed his hands together. "Get close and spread your legs a little."

I put my leg flush with Zack's, and he put his arm around my shoulders.

"I think you're enjoying this too much," I told my cousin.

I tried to focus on Sebastian, but I couldn't help but notice how big and strong Zack felt next to me. His body was warm, and he smelled good. I liked his arm around my shoulders a little more than I should.

Sebastian smirked and squinted up at us as he wrapped the rope around our legs. "Oh, I definitely am."

Once he was finished, he stepped away and said something to Tina.

"Line up everyone," she said. "And if you are caught deliberately spilling your drink, you'll automatically be in last place."

My mouth dropped open.

"See, I told you it was cheating," Zack whispered.

I stuck my tongue out at him, but he simply laughed and squeezed my shoulder.

While two judges stayed on our side, the other five judges went to the finish line, and Nelson directed them to use their phones to time us. Of course, Sebastian was our judge. I thought he liked knowing that Zack and I weren't really a couple.

"Are we starting with inside or outside leg?" Zack asked as he pulled his hand from my shoulders and put his palm out between us.

I linked my fingers with his. "Inside."

"Okay." He nodded once. "Let's win this."

Chapter Fifteen

BREE

NELSON PUT his hand in the air. "Ready, set...go." He swung his arm down, and Zack and I took off.

Inside, outside, inside, outside.

"Go faster," Zack said.

"I'll spill."

"No, you won't. Keep your hand steady. You got this."

"Okay."

I let Zack pick up our pace. It was harder than I had expected, but I managed to keep my hand steady as we reached the end.

"Drink!" Sebastian said, and Zack and I tipped our glasses back.

The beer was cold, which was refreshing, but I feared that it was going to take me too long to drink it all. I could hear other contestants also drinking.

I paused and took a deep breath, only to see that Zack was done.

"Keep drinking," he told me and squeezed my hand.

I lifted my cup once again and swallowed the rest of my beer as fast as I could. Quickly, I flashed the empty glass to Sebastian to show him, and Zack and I went back the way we had come.

"Don't go too fast. We don't want to fall," I said.

Right at that moment, the couple next to us stumbled but caught themselves just in time. At least, that was what it looked like as Zack and I passed them.

We were almost to the end, and I had a gut feeling that we were going to make it.

"Let's sprint," I said.

"You sure?"

"Yes."

"Okay. Ready, set, go."

We completed the last few steps at a run and just stepped over the line when we fell. I wasn't sure who'd slipped first because it happened so fast. One second, I had been upright, and the next, I was on top of Zack.

I quickly lifted my head to look at Sebastian, who had already been waiting for us at the end.

"Twenty-six-point-ninety-one seconds. So far, you're the winners."

"Yes," I cheered as I rolled off of Zack.

He held up his hand, and I gave him a high five.

We untied ourselves and sat back on the grass to watch everyone else compete. In the end, we finished first out of Tina's group, but we came in second after a couple from Nelson's team.

I jumped up. "All right, what's next?"

Tina laughed. "Someone's eager."

"I can't let them win."

Zack stood up. "*We* can't let them win," he corrected.

The couple walked toward us.

"Bree and Zack, this is Eddie and Celia. Eddie is Nelson's brother, and Bree is my cousin."

I narrowed my eyes. "You might have won this round, but we're going home with that trophy."

Eddie laughed. "Your cousin is feisty," he said to Tina.

I had just met the guy, but I could tell he was cocky. I was pretty sure he was the one from the crowd who had yelled at Nelson earlier. Celia, however, seemed nice. She just smiled at us and shrugged.

"Just super competitive," Tina explained. She raised her voice. "Is everyone ready for race two?"

People cheered, but I looked up at Zack. "We're not going to let them win, right?"

"Hell no. We're taking them down."

We turned our attention to Tina as she explained the next game.

"We can't have a three-legged race and not a wheelbarrow race, am I right? You're going to go down the lane with one partner being the wheelbarrow and switch for the return trip."

I groaned at the same time Zack celebrated. "*Yes.*"

Yes? I had the upper body strength of a newborn baby.

"News flash: we're not going to win." I lifted my noodle arms and flexed, showing him my lack of muscle.

"Pfft. Don't worry about it." He flexed an arm, and I almost swallowed my tongue. "I can lift my weight and then some when I'm the wheelbarrow, and when it's your turn, I will carry your lower body to make your job as easy as possible."

"Yeah, I don't know about that."

Zack pointed to Eddie. "Look at him. He has a small torso. And his girlfriend looks like she's weak."

He had a point, but we weren't only competing against Eddie and Celia.

Zack put his finger under my chin and lifted it. "Trust me, okay?"

I bit my lip and nodded. "I don't think I have a choice."

He chuckled as we lined up. "Have more faith, babe."

"Whatever you say," I mumbled.

"Decide who is going first," Tina said, "and get into place."

"I'll go first," Zack and I both said at the same time.

"I'm going first," he said.

I shrugged. It didn't matter, I supposed. Either way, we weren't going to win.

"Everyone, get ready," Tina said.

Zack got onto his hands and swung his legs up for me to grab.

"Oof. You're heavy." I was half-joking.

He wasn't as heavy as I'd thought he was going to be, but he wasn't light. But he either hadn't heard me or was completely in race mode now.

"On your mark, get set...and go," Tina yelled.

Zack moved forward at a nice clip, his long arms eating up the distance. He also kept his legs surprisingly straight, which made it easy for me to keep my hold on him. Before I knew it, we made it to the end.

"Switch," Sebastian commanded as if we'd forgotten the rules, but there was no time to tell him how we already knew that.

I quickly dropped to the ground, and the second Zack had my legs, he told me to go. I didn't move as fast as he had, but I was steady and managed to hold myself up until the end.

I just crossed over the finish line when one of my hands slipped out from under me. I caught myself before I fell completely, but because I had stopped suddenly, Zack kept going forward.

His crotch ran right into mine, and I squeaked out a sound.

Is he hard?

It had only been for a second, but I swore I'd felt penis in between my legs.

Not that it mattered because Sebastian yelled, "Time," and Zack dropped my ankles.

I rolled onto my back to see the two men high-fiving. Zack apparently had no idea his dick had just touched my lady bits.

He turned his eyes to me, grinning from ear to ear. He held out his hand. "I told you we could do it."

I let him pull me up. "I guess we'll see after everyone is finished."

His brow furrowed. "You okay? You don't seem very thrilled."

"Nope, I'm fine." I slapped him on the upper arm. "You did good."

He snorted. "I did awesome."

And he was right because we ended up winning by six seconds.

The next game was to carry a hard-boiled egg on a spoon and not drop it. Zack went down one way and passed it off to me, and I went back up the lane. We won that round too.

The last game was similar to the first. We had to carry a full glass in our hands while we held a balloon between our heads.

As we filled our cups, I compared our statures. I wasn't that short, but Zack wasn't going to be able to walk upright.

"We're not going to win," I told him.

"Don't say that."

"Eddie and his girlfriend are much closer in height than we are. They have the advantage."

"We can still win."

"If you say so," I told him, but I had my doubts.

———

It turned out, I was right.

"It looks like Eddie and Celia won by two seconds," Nelson announced.

Celia started jumping up and down, and I tried not to

feel too crappy. At the end of the day, this was all just fun and games.

"So, while my beautiful bride does some math and figures out which team won, we still need to figure out who to give our awesome trophy to since Eddie and Celia won two games and Bree and Zack won two games." He looked over at Tina. "How should we decide the winner? Add up all their times, and the lowest wins?"

Tina shrugged. "Sure."

Sebastian stepped forward and held up his finger. "I have an idea."

"What is it?" Nelson asked.

Sebastian moved in close and spoke quietly to the other man. When he was finished, he stepped back, turned, and smiled at me.

Uh-oh.

My stomach sank.

By the look on his face, I knew I wasn't going to like this.

"Sebastian has an idea on how to break the tie that is a lot more fun than calculating a bunch of numbers."

What did you do? I mouthed to my cousin.

He lifted a shoulder and grinned.

"We're going to have a kissing contest," Nelson announced. "Whichever couple kisses the longest and keeps their lips touching wins."

Oh crap.

Chapter Sixteen

BREE

KISSING?

There was no way we could participate in this tiebreaker. Coming into this, I'd realized that he was my pretend boyfriend, so we'd need to act affectionately toward one another during this charade. I'd even considered there might be a peck or two this weekend, but this went far beyond that.

I needed to shut this down as much as it pained me to let Eddie win.

I put my hand on Zack's arm. "I don't—"

"Start kissing...now," Nelson commanded before I could finish my sentence, and Zack pulled me into his arms and planted his beautiful lips right on mine.

At first, I stood frozen in shock, unsure of what to do.

But then Zack's mouth slanted over mine, and he licked my bottom lip. I only had so much willpower, and there was a hot, sexy man kissing me. His tongue caressed mine, and I groaned.

I pushed our bodies closer as his hands slid down my back to my ass. He squeezed my butt and pulled my hips toward his. There was no mistaking the hard shape of his dick as it pressed into my pelvis. There was also no mistaking the size, and a fantasy of Zack, naked and pushing into me, flashed behind my eyes.

I could just imagine how good it would feel.

And speaking of feeling good...

I trailed one of my hands over his neck, down his chest, and—

Zack pulled back, releasing me, and grinned. "We did it."

My brow furrowed, and I felt disoriented. *Did I miss something?*

Nelson and Tina approached us.

"Congratulations," Tina said and handed me the trophy.

"Uh...thank you," I said.

It didn't take a genius to figure out that Zack and I had won the tiebreaker, but I hadn't heard a thing or noticed anything after we were told to start kissing.

Nelson opened his wallet and pulled out two crisp hundred-dollar bills. "And here is your reward money." He waved it back and forth before giving it to Zack.

Finally, my senses were starting to return, and I told him, "Half of that is mine," as I swiped one of the bills out of Zack's grip.

"Hey. No need to be so violent."

"Sorry," I told him, except I wasn't. I was a little perturbed that while I hadn't even heard the command to stop kissing, he didn't seem the least bit fazed.

And yeah, he'd had an erection, but he was a manwhore. He probably got one if a stiff breeze blew past him.

And this was why kissing him had been a terrible idea. Since it was too late to change my mind now, I was going to have to use my money to buy myself something pretty.

Maybe a new vibrator.

I knew just the one. I had a coworker who was part of a multilevel marketing business that sold sex toys, and she always told me and the other ladies at work when she found a good one. If I purchased the one I'd been interested in, I wouldn't ever need a man.

"Why are you grinning like that?"

I looked up at Zack. "Huh?"

I hadn't even noticed that Tina and Nelson had walked away.

"You look like the cat that ate the canary. What's up?"

I lost my smile. I was not telling him that I was spending my hundred dollars on a vibrator because his kiss had made me think of hot, sweaty sex.

"Just picturing the new shoes I'm going to buy with my prize money," I lied. "You?"

He shrugged. "I haven't decided yet."

"Cool. Shall we get out of here?" I needed to go dunk my head in the lake or something.

"We need to find out which family side won."

"Oh, right." I glanced at Tina, and by the looks of it, it looked like she was still busy adding. "So, how did we win the trophy and money?" I hoped he wouldn't notice that I didn't know what had happened.

Zack frowned in confusion. "What do you mean?"

"I mean, you and I aren't really a thing, but Celia and Eddie are actually dating. How did we beat them?"

A slow smile spread across his face. "You don't know?"

Oh shit. He was onto me.

"Never mind. Forget I asked." I sure hoped Tina finished fast.

"It's okay. I'll tell you."

"If you must," I said, not meeting his eyes.

Zack laughed. "Everyone was cheering for us, and I'm guessing Eddie got jealous because he bit his girlfriend's lip."

"Bullshit." There was no way I'd missed people clapping and whatnot.

"I shit you not." He threw his arm around me and pulled me to his chest. "You are an ego boost though."

I pushed against his chest. "How so?"

He wouldn't let me go.

"I'm such a good kisser that you didn't even realize we'd won."

"That's it. I'm not waiting."

I shoved him again, this time pushing the trophy into his skin, and he let me go. I spun around and headed for anywhere but there.

"Denial's the first sign that you have a problem," he yelled after me.

He was right, but I needed a moment or two alone.

I heard footsteps rushing up behind me and sighed. I didn't understand why he couldn't give me some space.

Except it wasn't Zack, and when I saw Leah run up next to me, I was disappointed it wasn't him.

"You okay?" she asked.

"Yeah, I'm fine," I said with a fake smile.

I was going to have to tell Zack to head home. Having him there was starting to be more of a problem than being alone at a family wedding. I would have to tell my mom that we'd had a fight. She couldn't bug me too much if she thought I still had a boyfriend.

I took a big breath and released some of the stress I'd been holding. Having a solution to my problem made me feel a whole lot better.

"That's good. I was worried when you took off before we heard the results."

"Oh..." I needed a good excuse. "I just have to use the bathroom, is all. It couldn't wait."

"Yeah, Tina and Nelson weren't really thinking when they had us drink and had the party outside, away from the bathrooms."

"You can say that again. It was fun, and I am buzzed, but—"

"What's wrong?"

"I'm buzzed."

Leah's brow furrowed. "Yeah, you just said that."

I cracked up, laughing as everything came together. That was why I hadn't been paying attention to anything but the kiss. The alcohol in my system.

The amount of relief I'd felt a moment ago at deciding to send Zack home was nothing compared to how I felt now. I wouldn't have to send Zack home. I just needed to make sure not to drink around him.

Problem solved.

I looked over at Leah and realized by the look she was giving me that I hadn't said anything for a while.

"I'm sorry. I had a moment of clarification about something."

"Everything all right?"

"Better than all right."

"That's wonderful news."

"It is." I stopped walking. "In fact, I think I'm ready to go back and find out who the winner is."

"Uh...don't you have to go use the bathroom first?"

Whoops. I'd already forgotten. Maybe I was tipsier than I'd thought, which only verified my theory.

"Right. Let's go to the bathroom and then head back."

I looked over my shoulder to find Zack in the crowd. It took a second, but I found him talking to Elliot, and I smiled.

I was glad our time together wasn't over.

But I probably shouldn't be feeling that way.

Chapter Seventeen

ZACK

I REALLY NEEDED to get out of this cabin soon.

I grabbed my cell from my chest for what felt like the hundredth time as I lay on the couch and waited for Bree to finish getting dressed for the rehearsal dinner.

Her mother had gone to the actual rehearsal, so it was just Bree and me, and it was becoming a struggle for me not to go into the bedroom, push her onto the bed, and do things to drive her wild.

It was a good thing Tina's side of the family had won the contest because I was going to need some alcohol as soon as we got to dinner. I was hoping to drink away the memory of how she'd kissed me earlier that afternoon.

Swiping my thumb up on my phone, I pretty much ignored every post that scrolled in front of my face, so it was a good thing Bree finally came out of the bedroom, and we could leave.

She walked over to me, wearing a white dress that showed off a nice amount of cleavage.

"How do I look? Nice enough for a rehearsal dinner?"

Sitting up, I said, "I wouldn't know. Rehearsal dinners aren't exactly my specialty." I pointed to her clothes. "I thought you said you didn't have anything dressy to wear for the wedding. Or is this an outfit you forgot?"

She looked down at me with a horrified look on her face.

"What?" I didn't get it.

"First of all, this is a sundress that shows too much boob. It's too casual for a wedding."

I scoffed, "Says who?"

"And it's white, Zack."

I lifted a shoulder. "So?"

"Only the bride is allowed to wear white to a wedding."

"Oh."

She shook her head in horror. "Seriously, it's a good thing you're not really my boyfriend. You need a lot of training." She smirked.

"You're funny." I held out my arms, so she could take in my clothes. "Do I need to change?" I had on dark gray shorts and a white polo. I had actually asked my sister what I should bring, but maybe Tessa had been wrong.

"No. You look good."

"So, maybe I don't need so much training." Not that I was planning to be her boyfriend.

She smiled. "Maybe not, but..."

"But what?"

"Your collar is flipped up on one side."

She leaned over to fix it, and I got a clear view down her dress.

God almighty.

She wasn't wearing a bra, and I caught a hint of nipple.

Close your eyes. Don't look at her.

Except now, I could smell her perfume and the scent of her feminine skin.

My eyes immediately came back open as she was straightening.

God. What I wouldn't give to lift the lower half of her dress, slip her panties off, have her slide her wet pussy over my now-hard cock, and kiss me the way she had earlier today.

My head dropped onto the back of the couch. The next forty-eight hours were going to be hard. Pun intended.

"Are you okay?" Bree asked.

"Yeah," I said with a sigh. *Just hornier than a teenage boy, but I'll live.*

She chuckled. "You sure? You don't sound okay."

I pushed myself off the couch, almost running her over. "I'll be fine." I managed to put a smile on my face. "You ready to go?"

"Sure. Just let me grab my purse."

———

The rehearsal dinner was in the same place we'd eaten breakfast that morning, except this time, the room was completely decorated—I assumed for tomorrow's wedding.

"Wow," Bree said. "I can't believe they did this in less than a day."

I didn't know much about decorations, but I knew enough to realize it had taken a lot of work. "It's pretty impressive."

"Bree. Zack."

We both turned to the sound of our names being called. It was her mother.

"Do you mind sitting with my mom?" Bree asked.

"No. That's why I'm here, right? To show your mom you have a man."

"Right." As we headed in that direction, she asked, "So, have you thought of what you're going to ask me to do for the return favor?"

Sex, sex, and more sex.

I shrugged. "I haven't thought a whole lot about it." I smiled. "But don't you worry. I'll think of something."

Because sex was definitely off the table. This "relationship" wasn't real. We were both faking, and according to her, I was a manwhore. She wasn't even interested in me.

"I'm sure you will," she said right before we reached her mom's table.

"How was the party?" Diana asked with a grin across her face.

We'd barely seen her earlier. She'd come home from

shopping, run into her bedroom to change, and left with a quick hello and good-bye, so she could get to the rehearsal.

Bree sighed. "I'm guessing you heard," she said as I pulled out her chair for her.

"That you two won?" Diana clapped her hands to her chest. "Yes, I did." She leaned forward as I sat next to Bree. "I'm so proud."

Bree's eyebrows rose. "You're proud that we won a trophy at a bachelor-slash-bachelorette party?"

Diana laughed. "No. I'm so happy that you have a man. I heard how steamy your kiss was."

"It was all in the name of winning, Mom."

"Winning, schwinning." She waved away Bree's reasoning. "Before you know it, I'll be sitting at your rehearsal dinner."

Bree's jaw clenched. "Okay, I can't do this tonight." She turned in her seat and looked around. "Are there servers around here? We were promised free drinks."

My eyes landed on the bar area when I glanced up. "I'll go get us something. Diana, do you want a drink?" I asked as I stood.

"No. I'm good."

"Bree? What can I get you?"

"White wine. No, wait." She bit her lip, and my mind went to sex again. "Ugh. I wasn't going to drink tonight."

That got my attention. I frowned. "Why?"

She stared at me for a few seconds, almost in a trance. She met my eyes. "You know what? Screw it. I'm going to have a Dark 'n' Stormy."

I smiled. "One Dark 'n' Stormy coming right up."

I went to the bar and ordered Bree's beverage for her and a beer for me, and I made sure to let the bartender know I was on the party's winning team. As he got the drinks together, I watched Bree and her mom. Diana looked animated and excited as she spoke while Bree looked stiff and uncomfortable.

It was really starting to sink in that there was a valid reason she had brought me with her.

"Here you go," the bartender said.

I slipped him a tip before heading back to the table. Bree's drink didn't even make it to the table. She grabbed it from my hand and took a long drink.

I sat down, put my arm on the back of her chair, and turned my attention to Diana. "How was shopping? Was there anything else to do in town?"

As Diana began to tell us about her day, Bree looked up at me. *Thank you*, she mouthed.

I lifted my drink in salute. That was what I was here for. The *only* thing I was here for, and I had better remember that.

Chapter Eighteen

BREE

MY MOTHER HADN'T SAID anything else about marriage or weddings, but I should have known not to let my guard down.

Zack had been able to keep my mom chatting until my aunt and uncle—Leah's parents—and Leah and Elliot came to sit with us.

Leah's father had just arrived that evening, so I introduced him to Zack. Then, the men started talking about something while the ladies had our own conversation.

The food was served, and dinner went smoothly. By the time the dishes were cleared, I'd had two drinks, and I was feeling better than when we'd first arrived at dinner.

But my mom just had to ruin it.

"Nelson seems like a nice guy," my uncle said. "It was generous of him to rent out the whole place for the weekend."

"It was very generous," I agreed. "But then again, it

made me feel like I needed to spend a little extra on their wedding present."

Leah and my aunt nodded in agreement.

"Same here," Leah said.

"Just think, honey," my mother said. "When it's your turn to get married, you can pick out all the fun things as wedding gifts."

As if that were the reason to have a wedding. If I was going to get married, I would do it for love, not for presents.

"Mom, I already own my place, which is fully furnished and decorated. I don't need to get married to get gifts."

She shrugged. "You might be surprised once you start making a list."

I took a long drink from my glass. "Yeah, well, don't hold your breath."

My mom leaned forward to look at Zack on the other side of me. "If you want to marry this one, you'd better tie her down and soon. She's kind of flighty when it comes to relationships."

The entire table went silent as I looked down into my lap and played with my drink.

Flighty? I guess wanting to be with someone who respects me is now flighty.

My face was on fire, and I couldn't look anyone in the eyes after that last comment.

I couldn't believe my mother had said that. As if I just dated and broke up with men for no reason. And then to say it in front of our family.

I couldn't decide if I wanted to pour my drink on my mother in rage or if I wanted to cry from hurt feelings. I felt some combination of both coming over me as I fumed.

Zack took my glass out of my hand and scooted his chair back.

I looked up enough to see him glance at everyone around the table—except my mom—and say, "Will you excuse Bree and me?"

"Of course," my aunt said.

Zack took my hand and gently tugged me up. I saw my cousin out of the corner of my eye, and Leah smiled sympathetically. She and I weren't super close, but she knew enough to know why I wasn't with my exes anymore.

"Where are you going?" my mom asked.

Zack pulled me close to him. "Somewhere that's not here," was all he said before he led me out of the banquet room.

He didn't say anything as we walked outside and headed down to the beach, which was fine by me. He still had ahold of my hand, and I tipped my head back to let the cool night air wash over my still-warm face after escaping that humiliating moment.

We kept walking, and I didn't really pay attention to where we were going until we ended up on the beach.

He nodded his head to one side. "Let's go this way."

There were people hanging around, probably wedding guests who had arrived but didn't go to the rehearsal dinner, and I didn't really feel like being around people at the moment.

I nodded in agreement, and we were soon alone with only the moon to keep us company.

"You know I don't think you're flighty, right?" Zack asked and squeezed my hand.

"Thank you. I just hope that my family feels the same." I looked over at him, and there was enough moonlight to see the pity in his eyes.

I didn't want pity.

I let go of his hand and began to walk backward toward the water. "I don't want to think about my mother and her old-fashioned, misogynistic way of thinking. I'd rather do something fun."

Zack slid his hands into his pockets and raised his brow. "Oh yeah? What's that?"

I reached under my dress, slid out of my thong, and held it up in the air. "It's a beautiful night. Let's go skinny-dipping." I dropped my underwear and spun to face the water.

"Uh...are you sure that's a good idea?"

I looked over my shoulder. "Are you telling me Mr. Manwhore is afraid to get naked in front of me?" I looked down at his crotch. "Is that the real reason you're single? Because no one wants a second helping of little Zack?"

He chuckled. "I know what you're doing, but it's not going to work. I am very secure in my bedroom skills, so this reverse-psychology thing you're trying on me is a waste of time." He reached for the hem of his polo and pulled it over his head. "If you think swimming is a good idea, then I'm all for it."

He came toward me, but instead of stopping, he kept going. When he was mere feet from the water, he dropped his shirt, kicked off his shoes, and pushed off his shorts. I saw his tight, round ass for only a few seconds before he slipped under the water.

The second his head disappeared, I yanked my dress off and dived in. I had been a big talker when I teased him about his penis size, but apparently, I was a hypocrite because I didn't want him to see me naked.

It was one thing to let a guy you were sleeping with see you in the nude. It was another to let a guy who you were *pretending* to sleep with see you sans clothes.

The coolness of the water shocked me because it was so warm out. However, it wasn't cold enough for me to get out of the water.

"Zack?"

"Behind you."

I spun around to see him standing with the water about hip deep. I could see the V-lines on his lower abdomen, and I wished the water were just a teeny bit lower.

I needed to distract myself from the fact that Zack was naked, that I was naked, and that we were all alone.

"Do you want to race?" I asked, going deeper so that I didn't have to crouch to keep my breasts submerged.

Zack snorted. "You want to do another race? After what we did today, I thought you'd want to relax."

I definitely didn't want to relax. I would rather race to see who orgasmed first, but swimming would have to do.

I cocked my head to the side. "Are you afraid you'll lose?" I teased.

He laughed. "Not even close."

"Then, let's race."

"How far? There are no buoys out here. How will we know when to stop?"

That was a good question.

"How about we swim out deep and whoever makes it back to shore first wins?"

He looked down at my chest and lifted his brow.

"I mean, until we can both touch the bottom of the lake."

He shrugged. "Let's do it. You lead the way. We'll start from where you decide."

I took off for deeper water, and soon, Zack was beside me.

"You know, if we're really going to race, the loser should have to give the winner a prize."

"Hmm...I think you have a point," I agreed. It was more fun to win if you got a prize.

"So, what do you want if you win?" he asked.

"Can you make my mother disappear?"

"Not legally."

"Okay, that idea's out." Coming up with something was harder than I'd thought it would be. "I know. If I win, tomorrow, you keep my mother away from me as much as you can, and don't let her be alone with me."

"Are you sure?"

"Yes. That way, I won't do anything illegal."

Zack's chuckle carried over the water and into the night.

"That includes sitting beside her at the wedding, so she can't whisper anything in my ear."

"Got it. Operation Keep Diana Away from Bree."

"Exactly."

I looked around and saw that we'd swum out a good distance. "I think this is far enough."

We turned and treaded water as we took in the distance to shore and planned our swimming.

"So, do you want to know what I want if I win?" Zack asked.

"Nah, you're not going to win."

What he didn't know was that I had been on the swim team in high school. I hadn't set any records, but I'd held my own.

He narrowed his eyes at me with suspicion. "You realize, if you don't object now, you can't object after I win."

"Works for me."

Because he wasn't going to win. And even though I was a little curious, I was simply going to ask him after we finished. I wanted to get into his head and make him think his prize didn't matter.

"Okay...don't say I didn't warn ya."

I met his eyes. "Are you ready to race or not?"

He laced his fingers together, stretched his hands out, and cracked his knuckles. "Let's do this."

"On your mark...get set...go!" I shouted and took off, ready to win.

Chapter Nineteen

BREE

IT WAS hard to get a good start when there was no wall to launch myself off of, but I tried my best.

Back in high school, I had done a mean backstroke, but I wasn't going to swim that way while naked. So, I chose my second-best stroke, which was freestyle. I kept my head down and breathed on the opposite side of Zack, so his position wouldn't get in my head.

I wasn't as fast as I had been more than a decade ago, and I was out of breath when I finished, but I was feeling pretty good as I planted my feet on the bottom.

Until I saw that Zack was already standing there.

What? No. No, no, no.

"No way you beat me."

He used both hands to slick his hair off his face. "It was close, but I did beat you."

"But, but, but...I was on the high school swim team."

He grinned. "And I was a lifeguard."

"Dammit, I should have asked you if you had any experience." I had gotten too arrogant. I hadn't even considered that my opponent would have skills too. Lesson learned.

"I guess I should have asked you the same thing."

"Not that it mattered. You won anyway," I muttered.

"Sorry."

I narrowed my eyes at him. "No, you're not."

"You're right. I'm not." He lifted his hands out of the water and rubbed them together. "So, are you ready to hear what I want as my prize?"

"Definitely not. But I don't have a choice, do I?"

"Nope," he said, emphasizing the *P*.

I sighed. "Okay. We might as well get it over with." I made a come-here motion. "Spit it out."

"Well, originally, I was going to say that I get to take the trophy home we won this afternoon."

I smiled. That wasn't so bad. I would give him the trophy. It was easier than what I had asked for.

"But..."

"But what?"

"But then you got too cocky, didn't want to hear what I had to say, so I changed my mind at the last minute."

"Or you changed your mind after you won," I said suspiciously.

He lifted a shoulder. "I guess you'll never know."

I gritted my teeth. He was right. And now, I was probably going to have to do something I really didn't want to do.

"Are you going to punish me now?" I asked. "Are you

going to make me go streaking or make me walk back to the cabin, naked?"

"Nothing like that."

That was a relief, but he hadn't said he wasn't going to penalize me.

"Tell me."

He stepped closer to me until only half a foot separated us. "You have to kiss me like you did this afternoon."

My first thought came out. "That's not a—" I stopped myself from saying *punishment* out loud. I quickly shook my head back and forth. I didn't want him to know that I wanted to kiss him again.

But he seemed to take it a different way.

Disappointment filled his eyes as he took a step back. "You're right. I should not coerce you into kissing me again. That's not honoring your consent, and I apologize." He made a frustrated noise that I was pretty sure was aimed at himself.

Suddenly, I saw this opportunity slipping away from me, and my pulse quickened.

"You can just give me the trophy. That was my original—"

Arching up onto my tippy-toes, I grabbed the back of his neck and pulled his mouth down to mine.

Just like that afternoon, I forgot all about why I shouldn't be kissing Zack and only thought about why I wanted to.

He wrapped his arms around me, pulling me close as

his tongue slipped into my mouth. He tasted like sin and man. Forbidden and sexy.

The warmth of his body was a contrast to the coolness of the water, and I leaned closer to him. His hard length pressed into my lower abdomen, and a shiver ran down my spine as I remembered we were both naked and alone.

But when Zack brushed his shaft back and forth on my belly, I noticed there was something different about him.

Breaking our kiss, I stood back on my heels and looked down. Of course, it was too dark to see through the water, and without a second thought, I reached for him.

He hissed when my hand locked around his dick, but I barely noticed because I was on a mission.

When I reached the head, I gasped, and my eyes shot up to his face.

He smiled coyly. "Surprise?"

I blinked up at him. "Your cock is pierced."

"Guilty."

By this time, I was touching him with both my hands. I could feel the piercing go all the way through from front to back.

I was not a blushing virgin and had been with my fair share of men, but I had never seen a penis with a piercing in real life, so my knowledge was limited.

"Is it a Prince Albert?" That was the only type I knew, but for some reason, I didn't think that was right.

"No, it's an apadravya."

"I want to see it," I said and let go of his penis to grab his hand, pulling him along behind me.

He chuckled. "I'm not about to tell a pretty woman no when she asks if she can see my dick."

We splashed through the water as I rushed toward the shore.

"Sit," I commanded and got down onto my knees in front of him.

He was long, thick, and smooth, and a barbell piercing went through the front and the back of his cock.

I shivered. That thing would hit my G-spot in missionary and doggy style.

"Did it hurt?"

He laughed. "Yes. But that was a long time ago. I got it in college."

That was a lot of lucky women who'd gotten to experience Zack's piercing. In more ways than one.

"Can I taste it?"

He made a gagging noise, like he was choking on something.

I looked up at him.

"You want to taste..."

"The piercing. You."

He closed his eyes for a second and groaned.

"You don't want me to?" I asked, disappointed.

He laughed in disbelief. "No, I want you to—way too much. But..."

"But?"

"But I wasn't prepared for a sexy, naked woman to be kneeling before me, asking if she could put her mouth on me." He brushed his thumb over my cheek. "I'm afraid I might embarrass myself. I don't know if I can hold back."

I grinned at the compliment and shrugged. "I never said you had to."

He groaned again, covered his eyes, and fell back into the sand.

I took that as a yes and licked the head of his shaft.

"*Fuck*," he yelped.

I tasted skin and metal, which didn't really surprise me but it was different. And I began to wonder if he would fit into my mouth.

Telling myself that right now was an excellent time to find out, I parted my lips and sucked him inside.

Chapter Twenty

ZACK

I HAD to clutch my hands together, so I wouldn't push Bree's head down on my dick the second she took me inside her mouth. I didn't want to ruin the moment or scare her away, but it didn't matter because she was the one who took me to the back of her throat.

"Goddammit," I yelled out, not caring if there was anyone out here to hear.

Bree definitely knew what she was doing in the bedroom, and I knew I wouldn't last long if she kept making love to my cock with her tongue.

When one of her hands went to my balls, I sat up.

She lifted her head and sat back on her heels. "You okay?" She tilted her head as her brow rose. "Did I do something you didn't like?" she asked me like she was a student, sitting at the front of the class, notebook out and ready to learn. She wasn't self-conscious; she just wanted to do her best, and it was sexy as hell.

"Not in the least." I grabbed her hand and pulled her toward me until she landed in my arms. "It's my turn to taste," I said and kissed her.

We both fell back into the sand, where I cupped the back of her head as I plunged my tongue into her mouth.

She was as vibrant and alive now as she had been earlier that afternoon. Truth be told, I had barely heard anything that was going on around us at the bachelor-bachelorette party when Bree kissed me. She had felt so good and tasted incredible that I blocked out almost everything but the two of us despite the crowded area.

If I hadn't practiced keeping one ear tuned into my parents coming home while I was screwing my girlfriend back in high school, who knew what would have happened today in front of the bride and groom's family and friends? Thankfully, that part of my brain I'd trained in high school was a primitive part of my makeup now, and I had stopped the kiss when it registered that we had won.

But now, we were out here, alone and naked, and I only had so much strength.

If someone didn't come along and interrupt us, I wasn't sure what was going to happen.

Bree moaned as she shifted her legs to each side of my waist and sat up.

Her breasts, which were neither too big nor too small, swayed under the moonlight, calling to me, so I sat up, too, and sucked one rosy tip into my mouth. It hardened against the roof of my mouth, so I flicked it with my tongue. It was almost as stiff as my cock that was trapped between our bodies.

"Zack," Bree said breathlessly, but I was having too much fun to answer.

She pulled at the back of my head.

"Zack."

I reluctantly released her nipple and looked up at her. Running my hands up her sides and over her back, I said, "You are so fucking amazing."

She smiled and slid her hand up my jaw. "I need you to listen to me."

"If I can suck on your tits again, I'll do whatever you want."

"God, I was hoping you'd say something like that."

She pushed hard enough that I fell back against the sand again but not hard enough to hurt, and I had to laugh at the determination in her eyes.

I cocked an eyebrow. "Oh?"

She leaned over me until our noses practically touched and got up on her knees. "Yes." Her warm palm enfolded my shaft. "Because I want to know what it feels like to fuck you and your piercing."

"Your wish is—*holy shit. Goddammit.*"

Bree hadn't even let me finish before she sank back down on me. This time, on my dick with her hot, wet pussy wrapped around it.

She clenched her eyes shut and bit her lip.

I grabbed on to her hips. "Shh...go slow. There's no rush."

Her eyes flipped open.

"Unless you want me to bust my nut right away, that is."

Her lip slid out from between her teeth, and she smiled. "Aren't you practically a professional at this? Zack, manwhore and semi-professional stud."

I snorted. "If you're trying to hurt my manly feelings, it's not going to work because this has nothing to do with my stamina and all about how good you feel around me."

She visibly swallowed as her inner muscles clenched around my cock.

And that was how I figured out Bree liked compliments.

I kissed her neck. "Rock your hips. How about we take it slow at first?"

She rotated her pelvis forward and back, gentle at first until she got used to me.

"Wow," she said, already breathless. "I can feel it."

She didn't have to tell me what *it* was.

I grinned. "That's the idea." That was the reason I had gotten the piercing back in college to begin with and why I never took it out.

She ground her hips into me as I ran my hands all over her body and drew her other nipple into my mouth.

Little mewling sounds soon erupted from the back of her throat, and I kissed my way up her neck. When I made it to her mouth, I kissed her as I wrapped my arms around her waist and encouraged her to ride me harder.

Her fingers dug into my back as she began to tighten around me.

I couldn't help but grin against her lips. I loved making women come, and I was particularly excited to watch and feel Bree explode around me.

Remembering the little tidbit I had picked up minutes earlier, I whispered, "Do you know how good your pussy feels? You're so hot and wet."

She moaned and clutched me tighter. I would have smiled at my accomplishment in arousing her further, except I hadn't said the words just for her. It was the complete truth.

I nipped at her neck. "I want you to come for me. Do you think you can do that?" I groaned. "Because I don't know how much longer I can hold on."

She grabbed my face in both her hands and put her forehead to mine. "I'll come when I'm good and ready," she said with a grin.

I smiled back. "Fuck, you are so damn hot."

And that seemed to be the last thing she needed to tip her over the edge. She slid her arms around my neck, seizing me in a tight grip as her pussy contracted hard around my cock. I practically saw stars as she exploded.

I let her ride out her orgasm as I clenched my jaw to keep from coming. I worried I was going to get a lecture from my dentist the next time I saw him.

I didn't want to interrupt her climax, but I was fully aware I didn't have a condom on, and I needed to pull out before I came.

I waited as long as I could, but she felt too amazing, and I grabbed her hips to lift her off of me. But she anchored her heels under my knees and squeezed her thighs together.

"Bree," I panted. "I don't have a rubber on, and I don't know how much longer I can hold off."

Then, she said the words that made me get off.

"I'm on the pill," she said in a low voice right next to my ear.

"Thank fuck," I muttered before I dropped back onto the sand, taking her with me. Hands still on her hips, I rocked her back and forth once before I arched my pelvis up and came inside her so hard that, this time, I really did see stars.

Chapter Twenty-One

BREE

AM *I really hiding in the bathroom?*

I stood, staring at the door and commanding myself to open it and stop being such a chickenshit.

So, Zack and I'd had sex. *It wasn't a big deal.* It had been the coming together of two consenting adults. I did not need to be weird about having to go into the bedroom we were sharing and sleeping next to him.

It wasn't a big deal, I repeated.

I shook out my limbs, tightened my towel, and let out a deep, calming breath. I could totally do this.

I twisted the knob and casually walked to our bedroom. My mom's door was closed, and for a split second, I forgot that I was upset with her. I wished for a minute that she were awake, so I could avoid any awkwardness with my fake date that had turned the corner into not-so-fake.

After we'd had sex on the beach—*I had sex with Zack on the beach!*—we'd put on our clothes and walked back to our cabin. In the dark of the night, it was sexy and freeing, but as soon as the lights from the resort came into view, our sexcapade suddenly seemed more real.

The second we made it to our cabin, I bolted for the bathroom without stopping for PJs, claiming I needed a shower. It wasn't really a lie. I wanted to wash the lake water and sand off me. I'd also made sure to clean between my legs, feeling ridiculous that I had let him come in me without a condom. The man was a confessed man-slut, and while I was sure he protected himself, I should not have taken any chances, no matter how badly I'd wanted to feel his dick piercing.

I stopped outside the door and pushed my back against the wall as a hot flash came over me at the memories.

That little piercing was everything I had thought it would be, and I already knew I wanted to feel it again. But having sex with Zack once was a mistake. Having sex with him again would be asking for trouble.

Right?

He was Tessa's brother. He didn't do relationships. I couldn't risk any complications. Although...I didn't want to marry the man. Maybe a noncommittal guy was what I needed to rebound from my last boyfriend.

I thought the biggest question of all was, why was I trying to figure this out tonight? It was not the time to solve life's biggest mysteries.

I chuckled at my overactive brain and shook my head.

"Bree?"

I stiffened. It seemed like Zack had heard me.

Time to face him.

I forced my body to relax and stepped around the corner before I chickened out and went to sleep with my mom. "Yeah?"

Zack was staring at his phone as he stood next to his suitcase. He looked up at me when I entered. "You done in the shower?"

"Yep."

"Great."

He flashed me a quick smile before picking up his towel from the end of the bed. His eyes were already back on his phone as he walked past me and out the door. Two seconds later, I heard the bathroom door shut and the shower turn on.

"Huh," I said out loud to the empty room.

I guessed I had been worried for nothing because the guy had barely glanced at me, and he definitely hadn't made it weird.

Unless him barely making eye contact and looking at his cell was the weird thing. Maybe he was just as nervous about being around me now.

"Bree, shut your brain up and stop overthinking," I commanded.

I looked at the empty mattress. I thought I just needed a good night's sleep.

Hanging my towel on the bedframe to dry, I found my pajamas in my bag.

After getting dressed, I turned off the light, and I climbed into bed. Trying to relax, I closed my eyes as I waited for Zack to return.

———

I hadn't realized I'd fallen asleep until I was awake again. It wasn't that late at night, but apparently, my orgasm from earlier had worn me out.

I wasn't sure what had woken me, but I heard movement from behind me on Zack's side of the bed and felt the covers being pulled down behind my back.

As the mattress dipped and covers went back up around me, he said, "Ah, this is much better than the beach."

I smiled. "I don't know. I kind of like getting sand stuck in every crack and crevice of my body."

"Then, I should have saved some for you. I think I washed enough down the shower drain to fill a jar," he said and rolled toward me. "What is this?" he asked as he plucked the side of my shirt.

"My pajamas," I said in an *isn't it obvious* tone. I looked over my shoulder even though the room was mostly dark. "Why?" My heart sped up. "Are you not wearing any?"

He took my hand and placed it on his washboard abs. "Nope. And you shouldn't be wearing any either."

And just like that, I was naked again. He had stripped off my bottoms and top in about ten seconds.

"I didn't realize we weren't done."

He chuckled. "Silly Bree." He kissed me. "We're just getting started."

Lowering his mouth to mine, he ran his hand up my leg until he found my center. I was already embarrassingly wet for him, but I did have enough common sense to realize we needed to talk about a few things before we had sex again.

"So, I know I said I was on the pill, but—"

He slid two fingers into me.

I hissed. "But we should probably use a condom from now on."

"From now on?"

Shit. Okay, that wording implied we would be doing this more than once. Or more than twice.

I couldn't think straight.

"Uh..." I licked my lips. "I meant, we should use a condom if we have sex again."

"Agreed, but we're not going to have sex."

That got my brain working again. "What?"

Pulling his hand away, Zack sat up and situated himself between my legs.

He picked up one of my hands and slapped something in it. "Not yet anyway. Hold on to this for me. I need to take care of something first."

He let go, and I lifted the item in my palm. It was a condom.

My brow furrowed. "What in the world do you have to take care of first?"

In one quick move, he was on his stomach and on the lower half of the bed.

"There wasn't any dessert at the rehearsal dinner, so I'm going to eat your pussy first." He grinned up at me. "Now, make sure you don't lose that condom because we're going to need it in about half an hour."

Chapter Twenty-Two

ZACK

BREE SIGHED for the second time, so I finally woke myself up enough to roll over to see if there was something wrong.

"You okay?"

She was sitting halfway up, leaning against the headboard with the bedsheet tucked under her armpits to cover herself.

"Did you get some bad news?" I asked, my eyes going to her phone that she was fiddling with in her hands.

"No," she said in a defeated tone. "My mom is out in the kitchen, and I don't want to face her right now. I'm still upset with her." She looked over at me. "I don't want to fight, but I also don't want her to think she can say stuff like that. It's just not the place or the time. The wedding is today, and I don't want there to be any tension, for my family's sake. It would be better to talk to her once we're back home." She stuck out her bottom lip. "But I really want coffee. Got any words of wisdom for me?"

I had something better.

I flipped the covers off of me and hopped out of bed. "How about you stay here, and I'll get the coffee for both of us?"

I reached for the door when Bree gasped. "Zack, you're naked. If you go out there, my mother will faint at the sight of you."

I chuckled. "Right." I slept nude at home and lived alone, so I was used to walking around my place without clothes. It seemed as though I was too used to it.

I spun on my heel to find something to put on, and out of the corner of my eye, I saw Bree tilt her head.

"You know..."

"Yeah?" I found the shorts and T-shirt I had worn to bed the first night.

"Maybe you should go there like that. Then, when my mom passes out, I can get my own coffee." She bit her lip in thought. "Just make sure you catch her, so she doesn't hit her head."

"So, you want me to catch your mom in my arms with my dick hanging out?" I asked as I pulled my shorts over my hips.

"Yes."

Pulling my shirt over my head, I said, "Not going to happen. The only person seeing my junk on this trip is you."

I reached the door again and realized that Bree hadn't

said anything else. I checked to make sure she was okay, and she had a wide-eyed look on her face.

"Is there something wrong?" I raised my brow. "Did you change your mind about the coffee?"

"Uh...no." She smiled. "I still want it. I *need* it."

"You're not scheming up some other idea to get rid of your mom, are you?"

"No."

I wasn't sure I believed her, but she was adorable, and it made me smile.

"Okay then." I opened the door. "I'll be right back."

The kitchen was clear when I walked out, and I beelined straight for the coffeepot. I filled up two mugs, and just when I thought I was going to escape seeing Diana, she walked out of her bedroom.

"Good morning, Zack."

I smiled politely. "Morning." I wasn't going to be rude to her, but I didn't think it was cool—the way she had talked to her daughter the night before.

"Where's Bree?"

"Still in bed." I lifted the mugs. "I was just on my way back to take her some coffee."

Diana frowned. "Is she mad at me?"

I blinked, unsure of what to say. There was no way I was getting in between a mother and daughter fight.

She sighed and rolled her eyes. "You don't need to answer. I already know she is."

I studied the older woman. I wasn't sure if the eye roll

was at herself for what she'd said last night or if it was directed at Bree for her reaction.

"I didn't mean to upset her. Sometimes, I open my mouth, and things come out."

It seemed the eye roll was directed at herself, and my shoulders relaxed. I hadn't realized how much it would have bothered me to find out she was disregarding Bree's feelings.

"When you're a parent, you'll understand."

My eyes widened. *A parent? God, I hope not.* I didn't mean *I hoped not* forever, but I wasn't ready to settle down and have kids. Not for a long, long time.

I had to fight not to curl my lip in front of my fake girlfriend's mom. I didn't want to cause more problems between the two women, but Diana must have seen the part of my expression I couldn't hide.

The good news was, she laughed and patted my arm. "I know you and Bree haven't been dating long, and I am jumping ahead."

Jumping ahead? More like *getting on an airplane and flying to a new continent* ahead.

She stepped back. "I'll let you take Bree her coffee."

Grateful to get away from Diana, I headed back to the bedroom.

"Will you tell Bree I said I'm sorry?"

I pretended not to hear her. She could tell Bree she was sorry on her own.

I gently kicked the door closed behind me, and Bree looked up from her phone.

"My hero," she said when I handed her the cup.

"I'll add it to the list of favors I've done for you. You are going to owe me so big after this weekend is over," I teased as I walked around to my side of the bed and sat down.

"Put it on my tab." She lifted the coffee to her nose, closed her eyes, and inhaled. "This was worth it."

She'd had a similar look on her face last night when I was inside her, and I suddenly had to adjust my dick.

We'd had sex three times last night. I should not be as hard as the headboard behind me. I wondered what she would do if I tugged on the sheet covering her breasts. Would she let me fuck her with her mom in the other room?

My phone beeped on the nightstand, bringing me out of my sex-fueled thoughts.

I picked it up and checked the notification. "Finally."

Bree chuckled. "Sounds interesting."

Setting my cell down, I told her, "I had a guy message me last night and ask if I could start a job early. He wanted me to start today."

"When were you originally supposed to begin?"

"Two weeks from Monday."

She snorted. "So, not only did he ask you to start working two weeks early, but he also asked on a Friday night for you to start on Saturday?"

I took a long drink from my cup. "Yep."

"What did you tell him?"

"That I was busy. He replied that he was going to find someone else."

"Which he must not have."

"Just like I knew he wouldn't. Unless there's a cancellation, most electricians are going to be booked."

"When did this happen?" she asked. "I must have missed it."

"You were in the shower. Talk about ruining a postorgasmic mood."

She turned her eyes to mine. "Is that why we had sex again last night?"

I laughed. "No." A grin split across my face. "That was because it was too good not to do it again."

She looked away as her cheeks turned pink, and I was hard again.

"You know, since your mom is still out there, we could always do it again to kill some time."

Chapter Twenty-Three

BREE

AS TEMPTING as it was to get down and dirty with Zack again, I didn't want to do it with my mom in the other room.

There was a knock at the door.

"Bree, honey, can I talk to you?"

My eyes darted to Zack for help, but there really wasn't anything he could do for me.

"I just woke up, and I haven't had my coffee yet. Is it okay if we talk later?"

Frozen in place, Zack and I waited for my mother's response.

I heard her sigh and say, "Yes, that's fine. I'm going to breakfast. We'll catch up later." Her voice sounded disappointed, and I almost called her back. But now wasn't the time to talk about last night.

Her footsteps retreated from the door, and a couple minutes later, we heard her leave.

"Now, do you want to do it?"

I laughed and went to get up, only to realize that I was naked. I grabbed my towel at the end of the bed, wrapped it around myself, and stood. "I'm going to go shower. I want to make sure I'm ready in time for the wedding."

"Fine," he said with a dramatic sigh. "I will go find us some food while you do that."

———

I had done a good job of avoiding my mother the rest of the morning and the first half of the afternoon, but as soon as Zack and I walked into the room where the ceremony was being held, she spotted me and came over.

I stiffened as she approached even though I was pretty sure my mother wasn't going to say anything about last night in front of all these people.

Just as she reached us, Zack took my hand and squeezed.

"There you are. I feel like I haven't seen you all morning," my mother said.

That's because I made sure you wouldn't.

"We've been busy," was all I said as an explanation.

My mother smiled hesitantly. "Should we go and find the seats?"

"Sure." I didn't really want to sit next to her, but if I didn't, then I would be the one making the scene. Hopefully, the ceremony would start soon, and we wouldn't have to talk.

Chairs were set up on two sides for the bride and the groom, and we went to the bride's side. My mother went into a row first, and I went to follow, but Zack stopped me with his hand on my arm. I looked to him for an answer as to why, but he moved in front of me without a word.

"What are you doing?" I whispered.

We reached our seats, but before sitting down, he turned toward me. "Keeping you away from your mom today," he said as though it were obvious.

As we sat, I realized he had gotten my coffee for me this morning, and he'd kept me away from the cabin after we got ready.

"But I lost the bet. Besides, she's probably going to ask you to switch seats."

He put his arm around the back of my chair and his mouth next to my ear. "Since you gave me way more than the kiss I'd asked for"—he groaned softly—"I thought you deserved the help."

I clenched my thighs together as he turned to my mom while keeping his arm across my shoulders.

"Diana, I hope it's okay if I sit next to you. I figure the only thing better than having one beautiful woman next to me is having two."

My mother giggled like the teenager she wasn't, and just like that, she was putty in Zack's hands.

He smiled at me. "I think we're okay."

I rolled my eyes, but what I really wanted to do was kiss him. "I noticed. You sure are the charmer."

"That's why you brought me, baby."

Music started playing, and everyone quieted as the wedding commenced.

The groom came to the front of the church along with the person performing the ceremony. The bridesmaids and the groomsmen began to walk to the front in pairs, and when Tina came into view on her father's arm, I felt a pinch in my chest as we all stood to watch her walk down the aisle.

She looked so happy, and beauty radiated from her. I glanced to the front to peek at Nelson, and pure love shone from his eyes.

And I realized that tightness I felt was jealousy. And horror that my mother could possibly be right.

It wasn't as though I needed a man or a relationship to define me, but it also didn't mean that I didn't want someone to love me the way the bride and groom loved each other. At this point in my life, I couldn't even get someone to love me enough to not cheat on me, much less want to spend the rest of their life with me.

It didn't help that Zack was starting to feel more like a real date than a pretend one. He was being so supportive, and the sex last night had been phenomenal. I hoped I hadn't made a mistake in sleeping with him. It was ridiculous of me to gamble my heart on someone who could charm the pants off any woman he met.

I was glad my mother's and Zack's backs were in front of me, so they couldn't see me swipe the tear from under my eye.

I needed to rein in the emotions, or I was going to start sniffling and give myself away.

It seemed like forever, but Tina finally made it to the front and to her groom. The wedding was far from over, but the music stopped playing, and some of the specialness evaporated from the air.

The guests all sat as the officiant began his spiel.

Zack bumped his shoulder against mine. "You doing okay?" he whispered.

Oh no. What does my face show?

"Yeah. Why?"

"You just don't look happy."

I smiled and leaned toward him. "Don't tell anyone, but I think weddings are kind of boring. I hope this is fast, so we can get to the good stuff."

He grinned. "What's the good stuff?"

I shook my head with a laugh. "Drinks, food, and dancing."

He clicked his tongue and pretended to look disappointed. "Well, shit. I thought you were going to say something else."

It took some effort, but I put an innocent look on my face. "Oh? And what was that?"

His arm went around me again, and his lips brushed my ear. "As if you don't know. But just in case you don't, I'll remind you later."

I leaned back, looked him up and down, and said, "I guess we'll have to see, won't we?"

Chapter Twenty-Four

BREE

ZACK PULLED me into his arms and spun me around until I was laughing and dizzy.

A few seconds later, the song ended, and we came to a stop.

I collapsed against him, breathing hard as a slow song started up, and he wrapped his arms around me.

The reception dinner had gone well. With so many relatives around, I felt like I'd spent the whole time introducing Zack to everyone. I had to admit, this guy was a very good sport. No matter how many times I called him my boyfriend, he didn't flinch. He put everything into having my family believe that our relationship was real.

All night, he'd stuck by my side, held my hand, put his arm around me, and even kissed me a few times when he noticed people were watching.

And now, we were on what felt like our tenth song in a

row. It was a good thing that it was a slow dance because I was running out of energy.

We swayed to the music, and I looked up at him. "Thank you again for doing me this favor. Everyone loves you, and despite my mother's comment last night, this weekend has been refreshingly relaxing."

"I'm glad I could help. Have you thought about what you're going to tell your mom about me after the wedding?"

I sighed. "No. I mean, I'll tell her we broke up, but I'm not going to do it right away. I'm going to ride the high of having a boyfriend for a little while." I bit my lip. "Is that okay?"

He shrugged. "That's fine with me. But if I have to pretend to be someone else's boyfriend at another wedding, we'll have to break up."

He was joking, but the laugh that came out of me was completely forced. When I pictured him dancing with another woman, holding hands with another woman... sleeping with another woman...I didn't like the way it made me feel.

I stepped back and pulled myself from his arms.

Frowning, he asked, "What's wrong?"

Well, there was no way I was going to tell him that I was starting to like him as more than my friend's brother. I didn't want to ruin such a good night. And I'd been on both ends of unrequited feelings, and this side was by far the worst of the two.

I patted my throat. "I'm thirsty, is all. I'm going to go and get a drink."

"I'll go with. I could use some water."

I didn't want him to go with me. I wanted to get away from all his charisma for a few minutes, but telling him to go away would be a little mean.

We headed over to the nearest bar.

"What can I get you two?"

"I need a water and a beer," I said.

Zack raised his eyebrows. "I'll have the same as the lady."

"Coming right up."

The bartender gave us our waters first, which I almost finished in one long drink. It was good to know I hadn't been lying about being thirsty.

Unfortunately, Zack took the opportunity to roll up the sleeves of his dress shirt and unbutton the top of his collar, and then I was thirsty for something else.

Two clunks sounded behind us.

"Here are your beers."

I threw my water in the large garbage can next to the bar and snatched up my bottle.

"Hey."

I turned to see Sebastian approach us.

"Hey," I said back as he ordered something. "Where have you been?"

He pointed to the corner, where two pretty women were standing. "Talking to Tina's friends."

I rolled my eyes. "Talking? Right."

He grinned and lifted his drink to his lips. "I mean, I don't plan to talk to them all night."

"Sebastian, you're my cousin. Please stop."

He laughed and slapped his hand against the back of Zack's upper arm. "Hey, man, I'm not as young as I used to be. You should meet up with us later."

My jaw dropped. "Sebastian, he's my boyfriend."

He leaned in close to Zack and me. "But he's not your real boyfriend. Let the guy have a little fun."

I felt trapped. If I protested, would Zack know I didn't like the idea of him being with other women even though I had a valid reason for saying no? And if I told Zack to go ahead, I would feel awful the rest of the night.

I was really starting to regret sleeping with him.

I looked away as I pondered what to do when I spotted Leah.

Even better.

I looked back at the guys. "I'm going to go talk to Leah. I haven't seen her since last night at dinner." With that, I turned and walked away without giving either of the men an answer. I hoped that by not answering, it would let them think that I hadn't taken Sebastian seriously.

And if Zack did? It was just something I was going to have to live with.

I slid up to my female cousin. "How are you doing?"

She turned to me and smiled in sympathy. "How am *I* doing? What about you? I felt so bad for you last night."

I cringed. "Was it super awkward after I left?"

She chuckled. "A little."

"Did anyone say anything?"

"No. And if it helps, I think your mom felt bad after you left."

"Yeah, she wanted to talk to me this morning, but I put her off." I took a sip of my beer. "I'm just so tired of her hounding me all the time about getting married. It feels like it's all we talk about."

"I'm sorry." She looked over at Zack and Sebastian. "But at least you have Zack now." She bumped her hip into mine. "He obviously really likes you. He can't keep his eyes off of you."

That's because he's an excellent actor.

I looked over, and sure enough, Zack was looking my way, but the expression on his face was concern. I waved and smiled to let him know I was okay with whatever he decided to do.

I turned back to Leah. "Yeah, he's a good guy. But our relationship is new. And at this point, I'm so sick of my mother that part of me never wants to get married out of spite."

She laughed. "What is it about parents that brings out the little kids in us?" She leaned toward me. "My mother wanted me to wear this dress that she'd bought me for the wedding." Leah met my eyes. "It was so ugly, Bree." She shuddered. "But I couldn't tell her that, so I kind of brushed her off. But the woman sent me ten text messages, three emails, and one voice mail, telling me not to forget it. At that point, even if I had liked the dress, there was no way I was wearing it."

"What did you do?" I scanned her up and down.

"Oh, I'm not wearing it," she said and smiled coyly. "I told her I had to get it dry-cleaned first and that they lost it."

I burst out laughing. "I love it."

She curtsied. "Thank you."

"What did you really do with it? I hope it's not in the back of your closet because that will come back to bite you in the ass."

She waved her hand. "I donated it."

I tapped my temple. "Smart lady."

We stood there, talking for a few more minutes about our mothers and how alike they were when I figured it was time to find Zack again.

"I'd better go find the boyfriend," I said.

But when I turned around, he and Sebastian were no longer at the bar. And when I searched the room, I couldn't find either of them anywhere.

Even worse, the two women Sebastian had been talking to were gone too.

Chapter Twenty-Five

ZACK

SEBASTIAN HAD DRAGGED me away from the bar and brought me outside.

"What are we doing out here?" I asked him.

He shrugged. "I can only take so much family time. And if I can only take so much and I'm a part of that group, I figured that you could really use some time to get away."

That was considerate of him.

"Thanks. But your family isn't really that bad." A flash of last night's dinner came to mind. "Maybe Bree's mom could use a little work." I thought of my own mother. "But I suppose all moms have their own quirks."

"Yeah, she told me how her mother is always hounding her. It was nice of you to do her this favor."

"I didn't mind. She's friends with my sister, and I didn't have any other important plans this weekend."

"It was still nice of you."

I heard voices, and I looked over, expecting to see the

women Sebastian had mentioned earlier but it wasn't them.

I turned back to him. "Hey, you know that I can't hang out with those women, right?" I smiled. "I appreciate the offer, I guess, but I can't do that to Bree. If they're friends with the bride, I'm sure it would make it back to her mom eventually."

Plus, I didn't want to go anywhere with either of the ladies. I wanted to go back to the cabin and fuck Bree again. Ever since she had turned me down this morning, it was all I could think about. I was like some teenage boy on a hormone trip.

Sebastian laughed into his glass and took a drink. "Don't worry about it. I was totally messing with Bree."

I stifled my own laugh because I felt guilty for thinking it was funny. "Why?"

"She's like a sister to me, and since she's an only child, I made it my mission a long time ago to treat her like one. And living far away means that I have to make up for a lot of lost time when I do see her."

"Were you even talking to the chicks in the first place?"

He smirked. "For about two seconds."

This time, I couldn't hold in my chuckle. "You are evil."

He lifted an eyebrow. "You didn't ever do shit like that with your own sister?"

"Of course I did." I grinned at some of the memories that came to mind. "I think the best was when we were in high school and I told one of her boyfriends she had crabs."

Sebastian started coughing from laughing so hard. "What the hell, man?"

"Well, she'd told the girl I liked that I had VD. The girl never spoke to me again. My sister deserved it."

Sebastian was straight-up cracking up now. "Holy shit, I need to meet this sister."

"Maybe someday, you can."

Our laughter died down, and we stood in silence for a few seconds as we sipped our drinks.

"Can I say something, man?"

I looked over at the other guy, sensing I wasn't going to like what he had to say. "Nobody's stopping you."

"Now, I'm not saying my cousin likes you." He put his hand up. "Maybe you two are really good actors. But if I didn't know the truth, I would think you two were one hundred percent in a relationship. I know you're both adults, but like I said before, Bree's an only child, and I'm like the brother she never had. I don't want her getting hurt. Not after the last asshole she dated cheated on her."

I stepped back and exhaled the breath I hadn't realized I'd been holding. "Damn. I wasn't expecting that."

"She's family."

I nodded. "I understand. She told me about her ex, and I have no plans to hurt her. We both know this is not real."

"As long as you're sure."

"About an hour ago, we were discussing what she's going to say to her mom after the wedding to explain why we're no longer dating."

Sebastian's large shoulders relaxed. "Good, good."

"Not only that, but she has also made it very clear that she picked me to be her fake boyfriend because she doesn't want to have anything to do with me as far as a real relationship goes."

He winced and sucked air through his teeth. "Ouch."

"Yeah, so why aren't you going in there and asking her not to hurt me?" I joked, but it was a valid question. If I were some lonely sucker, I would have fallen in love with her last night.

A woman didn't just fuck a man the way she'd fucked me and then walk away.

Except they did. And I was okay with that. Or at least, I always had been when I was playing the field.

We talked a little more about him living in Indianapolis and possibly moving back to Minnesota when I realized that I had been out here for quite a while.

I pointed to the building behind me. "I'd better get back in there. I'm sure Bree's fine, but I did promise to be the buffer between her and her mother for the day."

"Understood."

"If you move back, look me up. We can go out for beers or something."

"Will do."

I liked Sebastian, and I hoped he'd take me up on that offer.

Once I was inside, I noticed the night had gotten to the point where the DJ was having people line dance. It was loud, the lights were low, and everyone was packed around the dance floor. I walked the perimeter, looking for Bree but couldn't find her.

I spotted her mother with one of Bree's aunts, so at least I knew she wasn't harassing Bree.

I walked around again until I saw her cousin Leah, who Bree had been talking to earlier.

"Hey, have you seen Bree?"

She looked at me with confusion in her eyes, so she either hadn't seen Bree or she hadn't heard me.

"Have you seen Bree?" I asked louder this time.

She shook her head.

Shit. It wasn't looking like I was going to find my fake girlfriend anytime soon.

I turned to go when Leah grabbed my arm. When I looked back at her, she pointed out to the dance floor.

I spun around and saw Bree dancing the Electric Slide. She had a grin on her face, and she looked beautiful out there, enjoying herself.

And I vaguely knew the real reason I'd told Sebastian I couldn't go with him and the two ladies, but I wasn't going to dwell on that now.

I had other things on my mind.

Impatiently, I waited until after the song was finished before I practically marched out to the dance floor.

When Bree spotted me, her eyebrows flew up, and her mouth dropped open.

I must have looked as determined as I felt.

Chapter Twenty-Six

BREE

ZACK SHUFFLED me into the bedroom and kicked the door closed behind him. It wasn't easy to see where we were going with our arms wrapped around each other and our mouths fused together.

Moments ago, I'd been dancing at the reception, staring at Zack as he stalked toward me.

I hadn't even realized he'd come back, and suddenly, there he had been, coming my way and looking like he was the hunter and I was the prey.

I'd licked my lips in anticipation as he reached me. "I thought you'd left."

"Nope," he'd said as he grabbed my hand and kept walking, weaving our way through the crowd, out the main door, and back to our cabin.

As soon as we'd made it through the front of our place, he'd pulled me into his arms.

And now, we were in the bedroom, where he gave me a

gentle push and I fell onto the bed. His hands immediately went up my dress. He pulled my underwear down my legs and off before he pushed his head right between my thighs.

His hot, wet tongue flicked across my clit on the first go, and I rotated my hips. When he sucked my bundle of nerves into his mouth, I started to ride his face.

Grabbing on to his hair, I told him, "I don't know where all this came from, but please, please don't stop."

He hummed around me, and I took that as a promise that he wouldn't dare.

I didn't know what had gotten into him, practically dragging me away from the dance floor, but it was hot as hell.

I tightened my grip on his hair as he did this vibrating thing with his tongue. White heat burst forth from my core out to the rest of my body, and I whimpered at the multiple sensations assaulting me. Not only did the guy have a cock piercing, but his tongue was also a built-in vibrator. I had struck man gold with Zack, and it only took me a few seconds before my first orgasm of the night exploded out of me.

When my muscles began to relax, he pulled himself from under my skirt and smirked down at me as he wiped his mouth on the back of his hand.

He didn't say a word as he picked up one of my feet and removed my shoe. Then, he did the same with the other, tossing them both toward the wall.

He dropped down over me, shoved his fist into my hair,

and kissed me. I tasted my sex on his tongue, and it was such a turn-on that I was ready to go all over again.

I hastily pulled my dress out of the way and went for his fly. I fumbled with his belt, and I grew impatient. So, when I finally got his hard length in my hand, I didn't want to wait a moment longer.

I wanted to feel that piercing hit me in all the right places all over again.

Dragging the head of his shaft through my wetness, I lifted my pelvis.

Zack tore his lips from mine. "Hold on there, babe."

He leaned over to go toward his nightstand, but neither of us had moved his cock before he did this, and as he lunged forward, he thrust into me.

I saw stars.

His length and girth stretched me, and his piercing hit my G-spot. I moaned as a tremor racked my body, and I dug my fingers into his back.

Zack froze, but his dick flexed, and I wrapped my legs around his ass.

I lifted my mouth to his ear. "Please, please don't stop. You feel so fucking good."

His body started shaking, as if he was holding himself back. "I don't have a condom on."

The way he'd said it, I knew it was more of an *asking permission* sort of thing than telling me we couldn't continue.

"I don't care. We've already done it once this way." I

squeezed my inner muscles, and he groaned. "Please," I whispered again.

"Fuck it."

Zack shifted himself into a better position, grabbed my hips, and pounded into me. I simply held on to him and let him take me.

The man knew what he was doing and just how to use the piece of jewelry on his manhood. He angled his lower body and went right for the sweet spot inside me.

I tried not to react as he rubbed my G-spot repeatedly. I didn't know why I was testing him, but I wanted to know how much he relied on a woman's signals.

I squeezed my eyes shut and tried to control my breathing, but Zack was too good.

He kissed me and nipped at my bottom lip.

I blinked my eyes open and met his stare.

"You can come now."

The heat in his eyes and his confidence were so hot that the only thing I could do was let my second climax take complete control of my body.

My back stiffened as I threw my head back, and I was vaguely aware of Zack slamming into me two more times before he emptied himself inside me.

After, we lay there, a pile of limbs and heaving chests. Zack rolled to the side, withdrawing from my body, and I whimpered from the feel of him leaving.

I put a hand between my legs, feeling his seed slowly leak from inside me. The blow job I had given him last night came back to me, and I slowly brought my fingers to my lips and sucked his cum from them.

"Oh my God."

My head whipped in his direction, and my face immediately heated. I'd kind of forgotten he was there and probably watching me.

"Uh..." I struggled to find the words to tell him that I'd just wanted to taste him again to see if it was as good as last night.

"So, do I?" he asked, his voice low.

I furrowed my brow. "Do you what?"

The corner of his mouth lifted. "Do I taste as good as you remembered?"

A small gasp left my mouth. I must have spoken out loud.

Zack swiped his thumb over my lips. "So, do I?"

I nodded slowly, still in a daze.

"Good, because so do you."

He scooted to the end of the bed, his body still in his dress shirt and dress pants. Even though they were wrinkled now, he was still so sexy. But that could have been the way he moved and the confidence he exuded.

Turning to face me, he said, "Do you need help with that dress?" He started unbuttoning his shirt. "Because you know we're doing this again, right?"

I scrambled to my knees, unzipped the side zipper, and pulled it over my head. With a flick of my wrist, my bra was halfway across the room while Zack was still undressing.

I wanted to touch him all over, and I was a little impatient.

I reached for his shirt to teasingly pull it apart, but I guessed I didn't know my own strength because the buttons popped off and flew onto the floor.

I gasped and tried not to laugh as Zack stared down at his now-ruined shirt.

I pursed my lips together and tried to keep a straight face. "Oh shit. I am so sorry."

He lifted his eyes. "But are you?"

I couldn't hold back my smile any longer. "Yes. But if you want someone to blame, you should really blame yourself."

"Really?"

"Yes. If you weren't so goddamn sexy, I wouldn't be so impatient."

He grinned. "I guess I am totally at fault then. My bad." He shoved his ruined shirt aside and pushed his pants off his legs.

As soon as his socks were stripped from his body, I grabbed on to his semi-hard cock. "It's really not fair that you have this. It's better than my favorite vibrator."

He twitched in my hand and hardened fully. He wrapped his hand around mine. "I think it's plenty fair because no pussy compares to yours."

Chapter Twenty-Seven

BREE

I WOKE up before Zack again and quietly pulled my phone from my nightstand. His arm was around my waist, and his face was buried in my hair.

I knew this thing wasn't real, but I wanted to enjoy waking in someone's arms a little longer before reality set in.

Because the weekend was over and we were going home today. Not only was I going to say good-bye to Zack and his awesome dick, but I was also going to have to talk to my mother soon.

She'd come back late last night. I'd heard her pause at the bedroom door, but since the lights were out, she probably assumed we were sleeping. We weren't, and Zack needed to cover my mouth with his hand as he brought the two of us to completion.

He felt so good that even my mother's presence didn't bother me.

We'd both fallen asleep after that, and that was all I remembered.

But now, the reality of life was upon me.

With a sigh, I snuggled back into Zack a little more as I unlocked my phone and relaxed.

Unfortunately, the quiet time didn't last long.

Soon, Zack began to stir, and I knew it was time to get up and get ready.

The morning flew by in a whirlwind of activity. As we packed, family members stopped by to say good-bye. We barely made it out of the cabin by checkout time.

By the time we got in Zack's SUV and on the road, I was ready to relax again.

So much so that I fell asleep and didn't wake up until we were almost to my house.

I yawned and rubbed my eyes. "Wow. I can't believe I slept so long."

Zack glanced at me. "You were tired." He smiled knowingly as he faced the road. "It's understandable."

I chuckled. "Except now, I won't go to bed tonight at a decent time, and I have to work in the morning."

"You can always call me if you can't go to sleep. I know a really good and natural way to induce sleep."

I laughed and shook my head because I knew he wasn't serious.

When we pulled into my driveway, it felt weird to be home. But that was probably because I didn't want to go to work the next day after having four days off in a row.

Zack went to shut off his SUV, and I stopped him with a hand on his arm.

"You don't have to help me. I can get my stuff."

He frowned. "Are you sure?"

"Yes. You've done so much for me already this weekend."

An eyebrow lifted in question, so I thought it best to clarify what I was thinking.

"You took time off of work, you put up with my mother and the rest of my family, and you played the perfect boyfriend. It was very nice of you."

He shrugged. "I didn't mind."

"That makes one of us."

He laughed.

"So, do you know what you want me to do for you in return? Because I seriously owe you." I had been thinking about this on and off all day, and I had no clue as to what Zack would want from me as a favor.

"Not yet."

"Really? You have to have some ideas."

"I could come up with something right now, but that's not what I want to do." He ran his hand over the steering wheel. "No, I want a favor for something that will be worth it."

I wasn't sure what that meant, but I guessed it meant he didn't want to waste it on something just to get it over with.

"Okay. I understand. I do really owe you. It makes

sense you'd want to make it count." I fiddled with the door handle. "You have my number, right?"

He nodded once. "Yep."

"Okay. We'll talk later then."

"Later."

I opened the door and slipped down from the seat. I pulled my stuff from the back and waved good-bye when I reached the front door. Zack didn't pull away though until I unlocked and pushed the door open.

And then it was just me.

I carried my bags to my room, unpacked, and threw a load of laundry in the washer. As I was cleaning out my fridge since I hadn't been there for a few days, my phone rang. It was Tessa.

"Hello?"

"Hey, how did the weekend go? How was my brother? Do you regret taking him? Did he hit on all the bridesmaids?"

I laughed. "I don't think Zack is that bad. You have to give him more credit. And he was a perfect gentleman."

Except when he had his penis in my vagina.

But Tessa didn't want to hear about that. And honestly, I wasn't sure how she would feel about me sleeping with her brother. She probably wouldn't care too much, but I could also imagine the lecture she would give me. Since I wasn't going to see Zack again until he needed a favor, it was probably best I kept the sex stuff to myself.

"There was no hitting on bridesmaids, and he really helped out when it came to my mom. There was only one time I wanted to wring her neck, so I would say, it was definitely worth it."

"Uh-oh, what did your mom do?"

I told Tessa all about the night of the rehearsal dinner, minus the *sex on the beach* part.

"Wow. Why doesn't she get it?"

I pulled a plastic container out of the fridge. "Honestly, I think she doesn't want to get it. Sometimes, I wonder if she wants me to be miserable in a marriage, like she was miserable." I opened the bowl and sniffed. Definitely garbage.

"I'm sorry, babe. I wish she were more understanding."

"Me too."

"So, did anything else happen?"

"Did Pru tell you how she accidentally told my cousin that Zack wasn't really my boyfriend? By the way, thanks again for getting my clothes for me."

Tessa laughed. "You're welcome. And yes, she told us about her slip. Although she blamed it completely on your cousin. She stands firm that if he hadn't snuck up behind her, she wouldn't have said anything."

"That sounds like Pru. She wasn't very impressed with Sebastian."

"I don't know about that. She also said he was too good-looking for his own good."

I laughed. I had sensed Pru thought Sebastian was attractive.

"Holding out on us that you have a hot cousin, huh?"

"He lives in Indianapolis," I said.

"Well, nuts."

"It's a good thing. Remember, we're part of the..." I could not remember the long fake club name we'd come up with for ourselves at dinner. That was almost two weeks ago. "You know, the we're part of the Hating Men Club thing."

"That's right." Tessa sighed. "Except sleeping with one every now and again is nice. I love my vibrator and all, but sometimes, I want the real D, if you know what I mean."

Having had the real D several times over the weekend, I knew exactly what she meant. Now, if I could stop thinking about the D and the owner of the D, that would be for the best.

Chapter Twenty-Eight

ZACK

"I DON'T KNOW how we're going to pick up any women tonight." Jeremy brought his beer to his lips and looked around the room. "This isn't exactly chick city."

It was the Friday after the wedding, and I had convinced my friends Jeremy and Matt to go to a local bar to drink and relax. I wasn't up for going downtown to a club tonight.

And I wasn't up for hitting on anyone or being hit on in return.

I shrugged. "Maybe we don't have to pick up anyone. Maybe we can play pool or darts."

Both of my friends looked at me like I was a stranger.

"You aren't looking for someone to have sex with?" Matt asked. "After doing that favor for your sister last weekend, I figured you'd be jonesing for some pussy by now."

Jeremy hit Matt in the upper arm. "I bet he already got laid this week."

"Ah, that explains it."

I sighed. "You know, I don't *need* to have sex all the time. And it's not like I am always looking to take someone home. Things just happen that way a lot."

Matt raised his eyebrows. "Right," he said skeptically.

"And I don't get laid any more than the two of you, so quit talking like I'm some sex machine who will die without it."

The two of them just laughed.

We did play some pool, and I thought the three of us were having a good time when a group of ladies walked over to watch us. Three ladies, to be exact. And it wasn't long before they started talking to us, and Jeremy and Matt returned the conversation.

I tried to be polite, but I really didn't want them around. I wasn't intending to be rude, but I just wanted a night out with my friends where we didn't have to try to impress anybody. And honestly, the thought of having sex with any of the women made my already-limp dick stay that way.

They were all good-looking and lovely. I just didn't want to get naked with any of them.

We finished our last game, and Jeremy pulled Matt and me into a huddle. "These ladies are ready to go, if you know what I'm saying. What do you two think about heading somewhere else with them?"

I pulled away. "Count me out. I think I'm going to head home."

Matt's and Jeremy's jaws dropped. I reached over and lifted both of their chins for them.

"Don't look so surprised."

"Who are you, and what have you done to Zack?" Matt asked.

I laughed. "I'm still the same person."

"Bullshit."

I shrugged. I was still me, and I wasn't about to argue with him about it.

Jeremy clasped his hands together. "Don't ditch us, man. The night is still young. And there's three of them and only two of us."

I clapped Jeremy on the back. "I'm sure you'll manage. You have a dick, a tongue, and two hands." I waved good-bye to the women in the corner and headed for the door.

"*Traitor.*"

I pulled my phone from my pocket as I walked toward my SUV. I'd only had a couple of beers over several hours, and I wasn't intoxicated. But the alcohol in my system was the only excuse I came up with for why I pulled up the number I did and dialed.

"Hello?" The voice on the other end was full of uncertainty.

"How's my favorite sister?"

"Uh-oh. What did you do?" Tess asked.

I scoffed, "Nothing. I was calling to see how you were doing."

"Zack, you don't call me to see how I am doing."

She was right. We were each other's only siblings, but we rarely talked on the phone with each other. We didn't even text one another that much.

I sighed. "You're right. I'm sorry to bother you."

"No, no, no. It's...fine. I'm just surprised, is all." Her voice lowered, as if she was trying to make sure no one else heard her. "Are you okay?"

I couldn't help but smile at my sister's concern. We might not talk all the time, but she really did love me.

"Yeah. I left some friends at the bar, but the night is still young, and I guess I'm not ready to go home yet. I can let you go though. I'm sure you're busy."

"Not really."

"Huh?"

"I'm not really that busy. I'm sitting at home, watching a movie. It's nothing exciting, but you're more than welcome to come over."

I hadn't realized how much I'd like the idea until she offered the invitation.

"Are you sure I'm not interrupting anything?" I asked, recalling her lowered voice. "You aren't on a date or something, are you?" My back stiffened as a thought occurred to me. "You don't need me to come over and kick out some asshole because he won't go home, do you?" My voice was hard as I pictured some prick harassing my little sister.

"No, no. I'm not dating anyone. Ever again."

That was new, but before I could say anything, she continued, "Just come over. I have popcorn, ice cream, and potato chips. If you want something else to eat, you'll have to bring it yourself."

I grinned. "All three sound delicious. I'll see you in a few."

———

It took me about fifteen minutes to get to my sister's place, and even though we weren't close, I knew it was safe for me to not knock before walking into her house. She was sitting in her recliner and waved at me when I entered.

"Hey, stud," she joked.

"Hey."

The couch faced away from the door, so when I first walked in, all I saw was the back of a head. I knew it was a female, but I wasn't expecting to see Bree turn around.

I also wasn't expecting the rush of excitement I felt at seeing her. I wouldn't realize until later that I felt a lot more from seeing her than I had when I saw the women back at the bar.

"Hey, Bree." I kicked off my shoes and walked around the couch since it was the only place to sit. Not that I was complaining.

Bree was half-sprawled out on the couch with a blanket covering her, and she had to pull her feet closer to her body, so I could sit on the other end. "Hi, Zack."

Falling back onto the cushion, I studied her face. She looked a little dazed.

I looked to Tessa. "Did you not tell Bree I was coming over?" I turned back to Bree. "Sorry if I ruined girls' night."

She shook her head. "No, it's fine. We were just watching movies and hanging out." A slow smile crossed over her face. "You're more than welcome to join us."

"As long as you share your blanket with me," I told her, picking up the end and pulling it over my lap.

The room was dark, except for a small light coming from the kitchen and the glow from the TV, but I thought it best to cover up. I was getting hard, just looking at Bree, and I didn't need either of them, especially my sister, to notice my erection.

I looked over at my sister. "So, what is this about you not dating ever again?"

"I'm too busy working toward getting the bakery started with Alexis. I don't have time for a man. And then once the business gets off the ground, I'm sure my life will be even more hectic." She smiled at Bree. "Besides, Bree and I and the others are part of the United She-Woman Single Ladies with Our Vibrators So We Never Have Another Bad Date or Experience Romance Again Because Men Suck Club."

"How do you remember the whole name?" Bree asked.

Tessa shrugged. "I have an excellent memory."

While those two were talking, I was trying to go back and process all the words my sister had said. I had caught the words *vibrators* and *club*. And something about *men suck*. "Hold up. I am so confused. What is this?"

The two women laughed as if I were a silly man who

didn't understand. They weren't wrong. But thankfully, Tessa took pity on me.

"It's a joke. The other night when you saw us at dinner, the seven of us decided we're sick of men and we aren't going to date anymore. We're going to die as spinsters."

"Ugh. *Spinster* is such a demeaning, old-fashioned word," Bree said. "We're going to die as badass single bitches."

The two of them were all smiles as they were having fun, but I was taken aback.

"Wait. I knew you were having troubles with your mom wanting you to get married. But you're saying you're not ever going to even date again?"

Chapter Twenty-Nine

ZACK

TESSA FROWNED. "Since when do you care if anybody dates? You are the definition of single."

I slouched down in my seat, crossed my arms, and threw my feet up onto the coffee table. "I don't."

Except that was a lie because I did care for some reason that Bree was saying she was never dating again.

The whole time we had been up at the lake resort, she had talked about getting out of a relationship not that long ago and that she didn't need the pressure from her mom. I'd thought she needed a fake boyfriend because she had ended the other relationship recently. I hadn't realized it was because she wanted to stay single. I really didn't understand why I didn't like the idea.

"Zack, are you okay?" Tessa asked.

I realized I was frowning, and I shook it off. "Yeah, I'm fine." I didn't want to talk about this anymore, so I changed the subject. "What movie are we watching?"

Bree and Tessa exchanged looks.

"We were going to watch a romcom, but you probably don't want to watch that," Tessa said.

"You don't have to change your movie for me. Watch away."

"You don't care?" Bree asked with her eyes wide in speculation.

"Not really. Honestly, I hope you picked a good one because some are better than others, but I'm cool with them."

Tessa picked up a remote. "Okay, as long as you're sure."

"I am."

She hit play, but the movie barely started before there was a knock at the front door, and two people walked in.

I recognized them as Isabelle and Elizabeth, two friends of Bree and Tessa. I didn't know them that well, but I remembered them being around back when I had been in high school.

Elizabeth cringed. "Is it okay if we crash the party?"

"Come in." Tessa waved her friends in.

Isabelle shucked off her shoes and walked farther into the room. "Ooh, is it movie time?" She walked over to the couch. "Scoot. I want to watch."

I looked at Bree. Her legs were still up on the seat. So, either she had to put her feet on the floor or she would have to put her feet on my lap. When she didn't make any indication she was going to move, I picked up her legs, shifted toward her, and set them on my lap.

"Sorry," I told Isabelle. "I hope that leaves you with enough room."

She grinned. "That's plenty," she said and dropped down beside me.

"Isabelle didn't get to watch movies and TV, growing up, so now, she's a screen-whore," Bree said.

"Guilty," Isabelle said. "If it's remotely good, I'll watch it. I am not picky."

Bree's bare calves were a little close to my junk, so I situated them better over my thighs. When I did this, I noticed how smooth they were, and I couldn't resist running my hands over them.

I tried not to think too much about how I would like to take these very same legs, push her knees up to her ears, and drive my cock into her.

I really wished the two of us were alone right now.

But since we weren't, I turned my focus to anything else in the room, and I noticed that Elizabeth was still standing.

Tessa noticed where my gaze had gone and looked up at her friend. "Are you going to stay?"

"Yeah. I'll grab a chair from the kitchen." She was back a few seconds later.

"Sorry my house isn't big enough. I wasn't expecting to have so much company. What brought you two over?"

"Elizabeth and I met up for dinner and talked about how we hadn't seen Bree since our monthly girls' night. We knew she was going to be here, and I wanted to see how last weekend went." Isabelle grinned at me. "And I'm so glad you're here too, Zack. Now, we get to hear both sides."

I turned my head to Bree. It was her story to tell more than mine.

"It went well." She met my eyes. "Wouldn't you say?"

"We got off to a rocky start, but yes, it went well."

Bree looked taken aback. "Rocky start? What are you talking about?"

"First, you forgot your wedding outfit."

She rolled her eyes. "This is true, but thanks to you, Tessa, and Pru, that was taken care of later that day." She raised her brow. "So, if that's all you have…"

I looked around the room at all the women to make sure I had their attention. "That was not the only thing. Bree wanted me to sleep on the hard, dirty cabin floor."

Out of the corner of my eye, I saw her mouth drop open.

"No, I didn't—I mean, yeah—" She sighed. "You're not telling them the whole story."

I laughed because, of course, I wasn't. I wanted everyone to feel sorry for me. That was what made it funny.

Bree sat up a little against the side of the couch, but she didn't pull her legs off me in anger, so I felt good that she knew I was playing around.

"What Zack is not telling you is that we had to share a cabin with my mother."

Isabelle gasped and leaned closer to me. "Oh man, that must have been awful."

Instinctively, I moved away because she was starting to crowd my personal space, and I didn't know her that well. As I did this, I noticed that Elizabeth was watching with an eagle eye, her expression somewhere between concerned and angry. I hoped she didn't think I would try anything with Isabelle, especially after just pretending to be Bree's boyfriend the weekend before.

"It wasn't great," Bree told Isabelle. "But because of this, Zack and I had to share a bed. He couldn't sleep on the couch because my mom would have wondered what was going on. And in the heat of the moment, I did ask Zack to sleep on the floor before I realized that it wouldn't be comfortable."

Isabelle wiggled her eyebrows. "Was there any hanky-panky?"

I burst out laughing at the antiquated term, and Bree blushed.

"Bree put pillows between us," I explained. It was true on the first night, and they didn't need to know what had happened on nights two or three. But I also couldn't resist teasing her some more. "But in the morning, she did wake up lying on me on my side of the bed." I put my hands up in surrender. "I was a perfect gentleman though."

Bree picked up a couch pillow from the floor and smacked me in the chest with it. "You were awake?"

I grinned at her. "Maybe."

She narrowed her eyes. "Don't believe him, ladies. He was not a gentleman because his hand was on my ass that morning."

"In my defense, I did that in my sleep."

Bree looked at Tessa. "You were right about him being a manwhore."

"I told ya."

We all laughed, and the conversation turned to us winning our trophy at the combination bachelor-bachelorette party and the awkward moment with Bree's mom at the rehearsal dinner.

"Have you talked to her yet?" I asked Bree.

She shook her head. "No. That's on my to-do list for tomorrow. And I am not looking forward to it."

Chapter Thirty

BREE

SATURDAY MORNING, I headed over to my mother's house. I didn't tell her I was coming, but I knew she would already be up and ready for the day. She never slept in, and after watching movies late at Tessa's place, I hadn't gotten up very early.

As I drove, I thought about Zack's unexpected visit. I hated to admit how happy I had been to see his face. I was definitely headed into *liking him* territory. But at least I was old enough to let my head run the show instead of my hormones.

But I guessed my head hadn't stopped him from running his hands all over my legs. I kept telling myself if he did anything more, I would call a halt to any more touching. But that was all that happened.

And then once the movie was over, everyone slowly put on their shoes and headed home. I had been wise enough not to leave at the same time Zack did in case a secret part of me hoped he would invite me over or something.

I couldn't be disappointed if I didn't put myself in a possibly disappointing situation in the first place.

Of course, that logic only seemed to apply when it came to men. Because what was about to happen with my mom was bound to be a huge disappointment.

But as much as she frustrated me, she did have many good qualities, and I did love her. And I knew she loved me. She just had a hard way of showing it sometimes.

I pulled into my mom's driveway and turned off and exited my car. I knocked on the front door, just in case she wasn't dressed or something, and then I walked into the house. "Mom?" I called out as I headed for the kitchen.

She met me halfway. "Bree. I didn't expect to see you this morning."

"I know. Do you have somewhere you have to go, or can you talk for a few minutes?"

She took a deep breath. "I can talk. Come into the kitchen first. Would you like some coffee?"

"Yes, please. But I can get it."

"No, it's fine. You sit."

I pulled out one of the stools at the island while my mother filled a cup for me. The fact that she wasn't looking at me made it easier for me to start this conversation.

"Mom, we need to talk about what you said at the rehearsal dinner last weekend."

Her shoulders slumped, but she didn't object as she brought over my mug.

And since she didn't say anything else, I continued, "You really embarrassed me. Not only in front of Zack, but in front of Leah, Elliot, and Aunt Maureen as well."

"I am so sorry, honey. I was trying to be funny and make a joke."

"At my expense. You weren't laughing with me, Mom; you were laughing at me."

She closed her eyes for a moment. "Trust me, I know this now. When the whole table goes silent, one tends to realize they've made a mistake."

I gave her a *no shit* look.

"I really am sorry. I regretted it as soon as the words came out."

I picked up my coffee and took a slow sip. I calmly set my mug back down. "What I don't understand is why you are so obsessed with me getting married."

"Obsessed?" She genuinely looked confused.

"I don't know what else you would call it. You want so badly for me to get hitched that you think it's better for me to stay with someone who makes me unhappy than for me to be alone. And I don't know where this all comes from."

Now that I had started, I didn't want to stop.

"I know you grew up in an entirely different generation than me and things were a lot different for you, but I don't need a man to take care of me. I don't need a man to pay for a roof over my head and to pay my bills." I jabbed myself in the chest. "I can do all that on my own." I threw my arms out wide. "I literally already do it all on my own."

I paused to take a calming breath in and out.

In a soothing voice, I said, "I just don't get it. Dad wasn't a great husband. He wasn't a very good dad either. Why do you want the same thing for me?"

My mother turned away and looked out the window. "I know he wasn't the best husband or father. But I still loved him. And we did have some happy times together. I know you don't understand the relationship I had with him, but that's okay. It was my relationship, and just because you don't understand it, it doesn't mean you need to judge me."

"Mom?"

She turned her head my way but didn't speak.

"What you just said there, that's how I feel. Just because you don't understand being single so long, it doesn't mean you have to judge me."

She sighed. "You are right. You are very right."

"You know, I told Leah that you put so much pressure on me to get married that part of me doesn't want to, just to spite you."

Mom's eyes widened in shock.

"Yeah. That's how much it drives me nuts."

She walked over to me and pushed my hair off my shoulder. "I'm sorry."

I smiled. "Thank you for the apology. I know it's going to be hard, but can you maybe try not to talk about marriage so much with me?"

"It will be hard, but I will try."

"Thank you." I picked up my cup and took another drink, feeling good and somewhat hopeful about this situation.

"Can I ask about Zack though?"

I winced behind my mug. Now, I felt guilty for lying to her.

"Yes, you can ask. Just don't ask if we're getting married."

She laughed. "I won't. I was just going to ask how he's doing. I really like the young man."

"He's good. I saw him last night at Tessa's, where we watched a movie."

I was very grateful for his spontaneous appearance because it gave me something to tell my mom.

I knew I was going to have to tell her soon that we broke up, but I really wanted to enjoy this little truce we had come to before I had to break her heart by saying I wasn't with Zack anymore.

"Do you think he would like to come to dinner with you soon?"

"Oh...um...yeah. And even if he can't come, I would like to."

"That's good to hear."

She walked over to the fridge, where she kept her calendar, and I knew she was going to ask about dates.

"Let me see when is good for him before we plan anything. I know he's starting a new job soon."

She looked disappointed, but she didn't push anything. "Okay. Let me know then."

"Will do."

Ugh. Breaking up with Zack might be harder than I'd thought it was going to be.

Chapter Thirty-One

ZACK

I WAS DRIVING BACK from the hardware store when my phone rang. It was my sister.

"Hello?"

"Hey, big brother."

"Hmm...two phone calls with each other in two days. This is the most we've talked in a month."

Tessa chuckled. "I know."

"Since you're calling me again so soon, I have a feeling it's about something that I'm not going to like."

"I don't know about that."

"I guess there is only one way to find out. What's going on?"

"Last night, when you and Bree were talking about your weekend together..."

"Yeah?"

"I didn't realize you'd slept in the same bed."

"Oh," was all I said because I didn't really know what

to say. "I mean, yes, but we didn't have a choice." Also, I didn't really know where this was going. "Why are you bringing this up?"

"Did you sleep with her?"

I frowned in confusion. "I already said I did, but we didn't have a choice."

"No, I mean, did you *sleep* with her?"

"Oh. *Oh.*" *Fuck. How to respond?* "Did you ask Bree this?"

"I'm asking you."

Relief rushed through me because this meant I didn't have to worry about giving my sister a matching story. Although I supposed if Bree had told my sister I'd had sex with her, the phone call might have gone a little differently.

I made a mental note that I needed to call her once I was off the phone with my sister to tell her what was said between the two of us.

But since Bree obviously hadn't said anything, I did the only thing I could do. I lied. "No. We did kiss a couple of times, but that's—"

"*You kissed?* You know kissing can lead to sex, Zack."

"No shit, Sherlock. But if you had let me finish, I would have explained that we did it in front of her family. I thought we talked about this last night with the bachelor-bachelorette party."

"No. Kissing didn't come up." She sounded ticked off.

I rolled my eyes. Bree was a grown woman. I thought

of her naked. A *very* grown woman. She didn't need my sister to play her keeper.

"We had to kiss to break the tie at the end of the competition. It was in front of a crowd of people. It wasn't a big deal. And I kissed her a couple of other times around her family. So they would think that we were a real couple. For Bree. Because you'd asked me to."

Tessa went silent for a moment. "You're right. I did ask you to do this for Bree." She sighed. "It's only that I worry about her. She's been cheated on by her last few boyfriends, and I don't want to see her hurt. And if she fell for you...oh man...she would get nothing but hurt."

"Hey."

My sister chuckled, but I didn't think it was funny.

"Zack, you sleep with a different woman every weekend. At least. I bet there are weekends you sleep with a woman on Friday and a different one on Saturday."

I gritted my teeth because she wasn't wrong.

I knew all the manwhore talk was just a tease, but I was really starting to hate the title.

"Yeah, well, I didn't sleep with any women this weekend."

"Good for you."

"Thank—"

"But the weekend's only half over. I'm sure you'll find someone by sunrise."

"I don't want to talk to you anymore."

Tessa laughed loudly into my ear. "Oh, Zack."

"What's that supposed to mean?"

"I don't know. I guess I thought you would take that as a compliment."

"Yeah, well, I don't. I don't sleep with women to make myself feel like a stud or to brag. I just like getting laid, okay? This is the twenty-first century. I thought slut-shaming—woman or man—was uncool."

"Okay. Sorry."

No, she wasn't.

"Listen, I have to go."

"Are you mad at me?"

I groaned. "No. But I am a little irritated."

She giggled. "Understood. Don't stay irritated forever, okay?"

"I won't."

"And let's hang out again sometime, all right?"

"All right."

"Bye."

"Bye."

I was no longer in the mood to call Bree after speaking with my sister, so I pulled into the nearest parking lot to text her.

> Me: Hey. Tessa just called me. She asked me if I slept with you.

I was going to send her another text, but she must have been by her phone because she replied before I could.

> Bree: OMG. Why would she ask that?

Me: Because she found out last night that we'd shared a bed last weekend.

Me: Don't worry. I told her we didn't.

Bree: Whew.

Whew? Yeah, obviously, I had lied, and I thought Bree would lie, too, but why *whew?*

Me: Ouch.

Bree: LOL. You and I both know we don't need Tessa asking a million questions.

She had a point.

Me: You're right.

Bree: Did she ask any other personal questions?

Me: I told her we kissed for the contest and a few times in front of your family, so they would think we were really together. She seemed really surprised by this. I'd thought kissing was a given.

Bree: It is what a lot of couples do. But thanks for letting me know. I'm sure she'll call me next.

Me: You're welcome. And good luck with your mom today.

Bree: It's already over and done with. It went well.

Me: Good to hear. Maybe someday, you can tell me about it.

Bree: Maybe.

Except we both knew that wasn't going to happen, and surprisingly, it made me a little sad.

Chapter Thirty-Two

ZACK

THE NEXT WEEK AND A HALF, I tried not to think about Bree. I really did.

I'd deleted her text messages after I told her my sister called me and asked questions. I even went out with my friends the next weekend to meet women. I met a few, but none of them did anything for me.

And because of this, I hadn't had sex for over two weeks.

I knew for some people, that wasn't a lot, but for me, it was.

Bree and Tessa were right. I really was a manwhore.

Except now, I was a manwhore who had gotten a taste of something different. Something he liked. And there wasn't a substitute.

Which was why I had asked Jeremy and Matt to go have beers and appetizers after work at the same place my sister had told me she was eating with her friends tonight.

It was a local Mexican restaurant, and because Margarita Monday and Taco Tuesday had passed, it was a slower night. When the three of us walked in, my sister and her friends were already seated at a couple of tables the staff had shoved together.

Tessa's mouth dropped open when she saw me. "What are you doing here?"

Her friends all turned to see who she was talking to, including Bree.

I looked around the place. "Um...eating. Or we will be soon." I slid in a quick smile to Bree.

"Ladies, you remember my brother, Zack. These are his two friends, Jeremy and Matt."

"You should come and sit with us," Isabelle said.

Tessa shot her a look.

"I agree," Alexis said.

I waited for Bree to agree, but she didn't say a word. My friends were for it though.

"Do you have room for us?" Matt asked.

"We can make room," Alexis said.

I looked at my sister. "Are we going to ruin your night if we sit at your table?"

"No," she said, but it was clear she'd be happier if we sat somewhere else. "It's going to be real hard to have our Man-Haters Club tonight though."

Jeremy and Matt froze.

"Man-haters?" Jeremy asked.

"Ignore her," Alexis said the same time a server came over.

"Will these gentlemen be joining you?" she asked.

"Unfortunately," Tessa said.

The server's eyes widened, and I took pity on her.

"I'm her brother."

"Oh," she said with a laugh. "I'll be back with some chairs."

A moment later, she was back with two other employees and three chairs.

"Where do you want them?"

"You can put one by me," Alexis said and scooted over.

Since she'd been sitting next to Bree until she moved, I quickly put my hand on the back of the chair, so I could sit next to her. As soon as I sat down, I wanted to touch her. She looked so professional in her knee-length skirt and blouse. I wanted to mess up her clothes.

I wanted to know if she tasted the same, smelled the same...and I wanted to know if she'd fuck me the same.

God, I miss sex.

"How are you?" I asked her as my two friends found spots to squeeze in.

She smiled at me. "Good. And you?"

"Good." I looked over to see if Tessa was paying attention to us before I asked, "Did my sister ever call you after I texted you?"

"Yes, but not until later that day. And she only teased me a little, so she must have taken you at your word."

"Wow. Imagine that."

She stifled a chuckle.

"Anything new with you?"

"Well, I guess I should let you know that we broke up."

"Oh." I'd almost forgotten that part. "How did your mom take it?"

"She wasn't happy, but she didn't say much, and for that, I'm grateful."

"That's good."

The waitress came back and took Matt's, Jeremy's, and my drink orders since she'd already gotten the women's before we got here.

After she left, Jeremy asked, "What are all of your names?" He grinned the same grin he used on women to get their panties off. "I'm Jeremy."

Pru spoke for the first time. "Yes, Tessa already introduced you."

I sniffled a snort. His smile hadn't worked on her.

"I'm Pru," she started, and everyone went around the table until they got to Bree.

"I'm Bree."

"Holy shit," Matt said. "Are you the same Bree that had Zack pretend to be your boyfriend?"

"Uh..." She straightened in her seat while I held my breath.

I had no idea where Matt was going with this.

"Yeah, that's me," she said. She looked at me and back to him. "Why?"

"Because Zacky boy has not been the same since he came home," Jeremy answered for Matt. "The dude hasn't gotten his di—"

"*Knock it off,*" I commanded, and everyone looked at

me. "Leave Bree alone," I said in a gentler tone. "I did it as a favor to my sister, okay?"

I was hoping that deflecting would get my two so-called friends off my back. I knew exactly where they had been headed with Bree. I didn't need the whole table to know I hadn't had sex since I'd gotten back.

Tessa, being the good person she was, turned the attention away from her friend. "Why don't you two mind your own business?"

Both Jeremy and Matt froze for a second, but as soon as all the ladies started laughing, they did too.

————

Dinner was winding down, and there was talk of people needing to get home so that they could go to bed and get ready for work the next morning, but I wasn't ready for the night to end. Even though I had to work the next day too.

I pulled my phone out and wrote out a quick text, but I didn't hit Send until I set it on my lap, out of the view of everyone.

I heard a chime off to the side of where Bree sat, and I crossed my fingers that she would pick up her phone before she left the restaurant.

Chapter Thirty-Three

BREE

MY PHONE'S text message alert went off, and since I'd been good about staying off it most of the night and most of us were finished eating, I figured it wouldn't be too rude to look.

I was surprised to see it was from Zack.

My gaze immediately went to him, but he was looking across the table.

Hmm. I had to guess he didn't want anyone to know he was messaging me.

> Zack: What are you doing after this?

I tapped my phone against my chin. *How to answer this?*

I could tell him I was going home to bed. I could string him along and pretend to not guess why he was asking me.

"No way," Jeremy said to someone else, and I remembered what he had said when he first arrived.

I knew just what to message back.

> Me: I think that depends.

I hit Send and pretended like I wasn't anxiously waiting for him to reply. All night, as he'd been sitting next to me, I had wanted to touch him. I knew I shouldn't. I knew he was bad news for me. And I'd thought he wouldn't want to have anything to do with me again.

But seeing the message from him that was meant for me only got my hopes up that he wanted something more from me.

> Zack: Depends on what?

> Me: Depends on what Jeremy was going to say when you cut him off.

He picked up his phone and sighed.

> Zack: I don't know.

> Me: But you have a good idea.

The sigh he'd just let out told me he did. I dared to make eye contact with him in front of everyone.

He shook his head slightly and looked down at his cell.

Zack: Fine. If I had to guess, he was going to say something about how I haven't gotten my dick wet since I got back from the weekend with you.

My jaw dropped, and I had to quickly close it and school my face to neutrality before someone asked me what was going on.

Me: Are you saying that you haven't had sex with anyone since we had sex?

Zack: Yes. And I am so hard right now that I think I'm going to explode.

I bit my lip as my breathing picked up.

Me: Is this why you asked what I am doing after dinner?

Zack: Yes. If you're not doing anything, is there a chance you'd let me take you home and fuck you? I am dying to get inside your pussy again.

Me: Yes.

Zack: Yes what?

His text came through right as I stood. I pulled my wallet out of my purse, grabbed some cash, and threw it on the table.

"What are you doing?" Pru asked.

"I have to go."

Tessa frowned. "Go? So soon?"

"Yes. I'll call you later." I looked around the table. "Thanks for dinner. It was nice meeting you two," I said to Zack's friends, and then I spun around and hurried to the front door and my vehicle.

As soon as I closed my car door, I told Zack to come over.

———

As hard as it was, I drove home at a normal speed because I didn't want to get pulled over for speeding even though it felt like I was going as fast as a tortoise.

I only had enough time to get home and pick up my kitchen and living room quickly before there was a knock at my door.

I didn't know why I was worried about my place being messy because as soon as I opened the door, Zack yanked me into his arms and practically carried me back into the house.

His mouth was hot and tasted like the salsa from dinner, and I couldn't get enough of his kisses. But more than that, I wanted to get down to the good stuff. Just like Zack, I hadn't had sex since the weekend of the wedding, and lately, my vibrator hadn't been cutting it.

But the fact that this man—this playboy—hadn't been with anyone since me made the fire inside me burn that much hotter.

Pulling him with me, I tried to lead him to my bedroom, but we crashed into my kitchen table, and my vase fell to the floor.

"Oh shit," Zack said.

"It's okay. It's metal, and the flowers are fake."

Not waiting for him to answer, I kissed him again, but he pulled away and grinned.

"Then, I think this place is just as good as any other."

Before I could ask what he meant, he spun me around.

"Hands on the table."

"Oh," I said, a little giddy.

As I bent over, I pushed back against his hard length and wiggled my ass. I couldn't wait to feel his cock inside me again.

"Someone's excited," he said.

"Nah. I'll just hang out here while you do your thing and contemplate life."

Zack laughed and pushed my skirt up and over my hips.

"My fucking God," he said with a groan.

I moved to stand up. "What—"

A hand landed on my back. "Don't you dare fucking move."

After he seemed to be content that I wasn't going anywhere, a single finger slid through the top of my underwear, just under the seam.

I grinned. I had forgotten I was wearing a lace thong, and I was pretty positive this was his reason for cursing. "You like?" I asked innocently.

"I freaking love." His finger, still under the thin strip of fabric that separated my two butt cheeks from one another, slowly slid down my ass until he reached my core. "Bree?"

"Yeah?"

He pushed two fingers into me, and I moaned.

"What were you saying about contemplating life?" He pressed down on my G-spot and rubbed.

My knees buckled, and I cried out. "I lied. The only thing I'm contemplating is how soon you can get inside of me."

I heard the sound of pants unzipping.

"Where are your condoms?"

"In my bedroom. But I don't want to wait."

"What the lady wants, the lady shall get."

Then, without another word, he pushed inside me, and there was a strong chance I saw heaven.

———

Later, as we lay in my bed, snuggling, Zack picked up my hand and laced our fingers together.

"I think I know what I want as my favor."

I'd almost forgotten about that. I looked up into his face. "Oh yeah? What's that?"

"Since I went with you to a family wedding, I thought you could come with me to a family reunion."

I saw the similarities, but I was still surprised. "Why would you need me to go with you?"

Neither he nor Tessa had ever said that his family was pressuring him to be with someone.

"Because I could really use you there." He cleared his throat. "I mean, I could really use a date there. I don't have the same problems that you do with your mom, but my grandma would love to see me bring someone."

For a second there, I'd thought that he wanted me to go with him because he wanted me there as *me*. Not that he wanted me there as fake-relationship woman.

"So, what do you say?" he asked.

"I say, that's a pretty easy favor to return. But I'm assuming Tessa will also be there?"

"She is my sister," he pointed out with a smile.

"Then, we'd better make sure she's on board."

Chapter Thirty-Four

BREE

I KISSED my way down Zack's stomach, heading toward my prize, when he threaded his fingers through my hair and groaned.

"Babe, that feels great, but my sister is going to be here soon."

I groaned, too, and rolled over onto my back. "But I want the dick." I stuck my lip out in an exaggerated pout.

"Bree, please don't make me say no to you."

Giving him a wicked grin, I wiggled my eyebrows.

"You are evil."

I laughed and threw off the covers. "What time is she coming?" I asked, deciding to give Zack a break.

"Ten." He looked over at his clock. "And it's already after nine thirty."

My eyes widened. "Oh, I'd better get out of here then."

It had been over a week since Zack had asked me to go

with him to his family reunion. Since that time, we'd spent a lot of nights together, but he still hadn't told Tessa I was going with him. The event was next Saturday, so it was probably time to get her up to speed.

We hadn't exactly told her we'd been spending time together, and I wasn't even sure what Zack and I were doing, but I knew I liked being around him. And he obviously liked being around me based on how often he texted, called, or showed up at my house.

I had to admit, the fact that he'd only been sleeping with me was quite flattering. But I wasn't letting myself read too much into it.

"I'll call you later and let you know how it goes," Zack said and kissed me on the mouth. "I'm going to take a quick shower before she gets here."

"Okay." I slapped his bare butt. "I'll see you later."

After I was finished dressing, I slipped on my shoes and grabbed my purse, only to hear the doorknob jiggle.

I froze.

There was a knock.

"Zack, open the door." It was Tessa, and she was early.

My brain kicked into gear, and I sprinted toward Zack's bathroom as quietly as possible.

I burst in just as he was stepping out of the shower.

"Holy shit, you scared me."

"Tessa's out there."

He frowned. "But she's early."

I snorted. "Oh, believe me, I know." I chewed on my

lip. "I hope she didn't notice my car parked across the street."

"I'm sure she didn't." His phone rang, and he went to the bedroom to get it. "Hello?" Pause. "I just got out of the shower. You're early." Pause. "I'll be there in a second. Let me get dressed." He hit End and looked at me. "We're supposed to go get coffee, so I'll try to get her out of here as soon as possible." He smiled sympathetically. "Are you going to be okay?"

I kicked off my shoes, piled some pillows against his headboard, and lay down. "I'll just scroll on my phone while I wait."

"I'm sorry."

"Don't be. It's not your fault."

He got dressed and kissed me again. "I'll see you later." He smiled. "This time, for real."

"Later. Have fun."

Zack left his bedroom and closed the door, leaving it open just a crack, which allowed me to hear what was going on down the hall.

I heard the door open and Tessa say hi.

"Shall we get going?" Zack asked her.

"Where are we going again?"

"To get coffee. There's a great place not far from here."

Tessa didn't answer right away. And when she did talk, she said, "You and I have only recently started seeing each other more outside Mom and Dad's, and the fact that you want to get coffee has me believing you want to talk to me about something. So, why don't you just spit it out?"

Tessa was smart, but I was still hoping that they would leave, so I could get out of there.

"Can we go and do this over coffee? Please? I haven't had any yet this morning."

"Zack, whatever you have to say can't be that big of a deal. Unless you need a kidney or part of my liver, but if it's that, then I want more than coffee. I want a steak dinner," she joked.

I couldn't be sure, but I think Zack sighed. "Fine. I just want to give you a heads-up that I am bringing Bree to our family reunion next weekend."

"What? Why?"

"Because I did a favor for her and she's doing a favor for me in return."

"But nobody in our family cares if you're with someone or not."

"Grandma does."

"Yeah, Grandma's like that with everyone. You're not being singled out."

"Maybe not, but she's still coming. I like Bree, and I want to bring her with me."

Warm fuzzies filled my belly. I liked hearing that he liked me even if he only meant it as a friend.

"And Bree is okay with this? She knows it's a favor for a favor?"

"Yes."

"Even so, I don't think this is a good idea."

"We're not asking for your opinion."

Tessa gasped loud enough for me to hear. "*We*? It's *we*

now? Zack, what are you doing with my friend?"

"What do you mean by that?"

"Oh my God, I need to talk to her."

Five seconds later, my phone rang.

Shit. I hadn't thought she'd meant she needed to talk to me right now.

I instantly rolled over to mask the sound of my cell going off while trying to push the volume button down.

"What the hell?" Tessa said, and I closed my eyes and winced.

"That's my phone," Zack said. His voice was amazingly calm, to the point where he almost sounded bored.

He came in the bedroom a few seconds later and gave me a wide-eyed look that said, *That was close.*

I mouthed, *I'm sorry.*

He smiled to let me know it was okay and was out the door again.

I hoped Tessa bought that it had been his phone ringing at the same time she dialed. Although she was probably going to wonder why I hadn't answered. At least if she called back now, I knew my phone wouldn't ring.

"I like Bree. She's my friend. I think you worry too much," Zack told Tessa as he made his way back to her.

I smiled when he said again that he liked me.

Tessa didn't answer.

"Do you want to go for that coffee now?" he asked.

"Sure. But don't think I'm not going to talk to her about this whole situation."

"I wouldn't expect anything less from you."

A moment later, I heard them leave, and I heaved a sigh of relief.

I waited a little bit before I called Tessa back. I knew they were going to have coffee, but I wasn't supposed to know that. I figured she would just ignore me and hit me up later.

"Hello?"

I was surprised she'd answered, and I almost didn't say anything right away.

"Hey. I saw you'd called. What's up?" I hoped I sounded as casual as I was trying to.

"Go on. I'll meet you inside," she said. She sounded like she had pulled her cell away from her mouth. "I'm having coffee with Zack this morning," she said to me now. "He said that you are coming to our family reunion as his date."

"Yes. I told him I would do something in return for him going to the wedding with me. Are you okay with that?"

She sighed. "Yes."

"But..."

"But he called you a *we*. I'm worried about you."

I laughed. "Zack and I spent a lot of time together during the wedding weekend. I consider him a friend now. Is that okay?"

"Hmm. That's what he said."

"What's that?" I asked even though I already knew.

"He said you two are friends."

"Is that okay? You know I like you more, right?" I joked.

She chuckled. "Yeah, it's okay. I just don't want you to get hurt."

"Why would you think that?"

"My brother...he's got a magnetic personality. And he's the type of person who makes everyone think they are special to him. I'm not saying he's doing it on purpose or that he's lying. He's genuinely a nice person, and I don't think he realizes how charismatic he is. I just don't want to see you get sucked up into that and end up having it mean more to you than it does to him."

I bit my lip as her words hit me hard. I could completely understand what she was saying about Zack, and I couldn't lie and say that a sliver of concern didn't go through me. But what Tessa didn't know was that the two of us had spent almost every night in each other's beds for the last week. That part wasn't something that could be faked or chalked up to personality.

"I can see what you mean. My mother loved him. But you don't need to worry about me. We're part of a club, remember?"

Tessa laughed. "Okay. I'd better go. He's waiting for me."

"Okay. Tell him I said hi."

"Will do. I'll talk to you later."

"Bye."

"Bye."

The phone call ended, and I lay back on Zack's bed. It felt good that I had reassured Tessa, but a part of me felt like I was lying.

And I knew it was because I liked Zack way more than a friend, and it did concern me that I might be getting in over my head.

Chapter Thirty-Five

BREE

"MOM, I'd like you to meet Bree."

Trudy Archer turned around at the sound of her son's voice and gave him a look like he was a pain in the butt but she loved him anyway.

"Yes. I know who Bree is." She shook her head at him and turned to me. "Hi, Bree. I didn't expect to see you here." She scanned the park where the family reunion was taking place. "Did you come with Tessa? I haven't seen her yet."

"Hi, Trudy," was all I said in response. I left it to Zack to explain why I was there.

"Actually, Mom, Bree is with me. We just started seeing each other."

Trudy grinned. "Really?" She clapped her hands together. "I love this for the two of you." She took a step in my direction and elbowed me gently. "I've been trying to get this boy to settle down for years," she said before resuming her spot in front of us.

I couldn't help but smile at her.

"How did it happen?" Trudy asked.

"Bree needed someone to go with her to her cousin's wedding, so her mom would get off her case about having a boyfriend, and things kind of progressed from there. I told her she owed me a family outing for a family outing," Zack told his mom while I stood, frozen with surprise.

Someone called Trudy's name.

"I'm going to go talk to your great-aunt," she said. "But tell me more about this wedding later." She took my hand and squeezed. "Tessa has told me your mother is hard on you. I'm glad Zack was there to help and that something developed out of it." She grinned and lifted her shoulders in almost giddiness before taking off.

Zack turned to me. "Why the shocked face, babe?"

I licked my dry lips. "I guess I was surprised you told your mom something so close to the truth. I mean, I almost believed it."

He leaned in and kissed me. "Bree, you and I have spent every night in each other's beds. If we're not seeing each other, what exactly do you think we're doing?"

"I—I—I—"

Zack laughed and pulled me into his arms. "I know you have your cool new club, but I kind of figured you were okay with us being a thing since you like me making you come so much, and vice versa."

My eyes darted around quickly, and my face heated even though I was pretty sure no one had heard him.

And I was more than okay with us being a thing. Up until then, I hadn't let myself think it could actually be true.

I wrinkled my nose at him. "I guess I'm okay with you telling people we're seeing each other," I teased him. "But in all seriousness, you and I did start this thing because your sister called you a manwhore." Looking down, I didn't want him to see the fear in my face. "Aren't you going to miss all the sex you had?"

He chuckled and lifted my chin. "I've had more sex the last two weeks than I did the whole month before I met you." He smiled. "I'm all good with the sex, babe." He slid a hand down to my ass and nudged me close, so I could feel his hard-on. "I'm all good." His words were a little slower this time.

"You are very naughty. We are in public, surrounded by your family."

He snorted. "That is not going to stop me from picturing you naked or thinking about how you rode me reverse cowgirl this morning."

"Zack." I pushed my face into his chest. "I can't believe you just said that."

"I can't believe that was the first time you rode me like that. You went off like a rocket."

I rubbed my nose up to his jawline and nibbled on his neck. "Stop talking like that, or I'll never do it again."

He laughed and squeezed me in an almost bear hug.

A throat cleared beside us.

Our heads swung in that direction, only to see Tessa standing there.

Oh shit.

All that talk of actually dating, and I'd forgotten that Tessa didn't know.

I stepped back from Zack. "Hey," I said weakly.

She looked at her brother with raised eyebrows and crossed arms. "I thought you were just friends." She shook her head in disbelief. "I knew something was up when you said *we*."

Zack grabbed my hand. "Fine. You figured it out. I like Bree, and she likes me. And we're dating now. Is that okay?"

"I'm just glad you two finally told me the truth."

My jaw dropped open.

"Oh, don't look so surprised," she said to me. "Your phone with my personal ringtone went off in my brother's *bedroom* last weekend. Also, I totally saw your car parked outside." She gave me a pointed look. "I am a little disappointed that you didn't tell me sooner though." Her bottom lip went out. "I thought we were friends."

"Honestly, I didn't know where your brother and I stood until today."

She smacked Zack in the stomach with the back of her hand, and a big whoosh of air flew out of his mouth.

"Dick."

"I practically live inside her. I thought she knew."

"Oh my God, Zack," I said the same time Tessa said,

"A woman needs words, Zack. We can't read your mind." She wrinkled her nose and stuck out the tip of her tongue. "Also...*gross*. No offense, Bree."

He stood up straight, rubbing his belly with a wince. "That's what you get for socking me in the gut."

"As long as you two are happy, I'm happy. But please, Zack, don't hurt this poor woman. She's been through enough."

"I don't plan to."

"Famous last words," Tessa said.

She had a point. I was sure none of my exes had started dating me with the intention of cheating and hurting me, and that did scare me a little. For some reason, I felt that Zack could hurt me more than any of the others had.

He put his arm around me. "Don't worry about my girl. I got her."

"*Our* girl," Tessa said. "She was mine first."

———

Even though Tess had echoed me with her worry, the more I heard Zack introduce me to his family as the woman he was seeing, the more my heart swelled.

I was getting a little tired from socializing and being the new person who had to be introduced to everyone in the group. Thankfully, the family reunion was a one-day event. I was going to have to give Zack props for spending a long weekend with mine. He hadn't complained once.

When I found myself left alone for a minute, I took the

chance to escape to the restroom. As far as being a restroom at a park, it was pretty clean, but it was still an outdoor restroom situation, so I tried to get in and out of there as fast as possible.

But right before I was going to flush, I heard a group of women walk in. One of them said something about Zack, and I froze.

"Can you believe Zack has a girlfriend?" the first woman said.

"I know. It's a good thing someone said something to me before I met her, so I was prepared. He hasn't brought a girl around in years," Woman Two said.

They hadn't said anything bad, but I knew they would be embarrassed if I walked out of the stall now.

"I am really surprised. Jay said he saw him not that long ago at a bar with a chick on each arm. Jay wasn't sure, but it seemed like he'd left with both of them," a third woman said.

And I knew Jay was Zack's cousin.

My stomach was beginning to knot. Even though Zack had spent the last two weekends with me and we hadn't even been official really until today, the thought of him having sex with two women tore me up. I could never compete with that.

"Yeah, Tessa always talks about how he sleeps around with whoever. I don't know...those men don't usually change. It's like they get a high off of women wanting them, and they can only achieve that high again with a different person."

I wasn't even sure who was speaking at this point because I felt sick.

Someone clicked their tongue in disappointment.

"And that Bree seems like a nice girl. I heard she's been friends with Tessa for years. I'm surprised she let her friend date her brother."

"Doesn't seem like she's being that good of a friend."

But Tessa had tried to warn me.

Oh God. I hoped they all left soon because I needed to get out of there.

"Oh, look. I got the stain out," one of the ladies said.

"Wonderful. Let's get out of here."

They filed out, and I waited as long as I could before I bolted from the restroom after washing up.

My instinct was to run away without a word, but I wasn't in high school any longer, so I went to find Zack.

Chapter Thirty-Six

ZACK

I CAUGHT sight of Bree leaving the restroom and approaching my sister. Whatever Bree said, Tessa seemed concerned. She nodded right before she headed in another direction, and then Bree came my way with a serious look on her face.

I met her halfway. "Hey, is everything okay?"

"I'm not feeling very well."

I moved toward her out of instinct, but she took a step back. I didn't read too much into it because if she didn't feel good, she probably didn't want anyone close to her. "Do you need me to take you home?"

"No. Tessa said I could take her car and she'll catch a ride with someone else. She went to grab her keys out of her purse."

"It's okay. I want to take you." I didn't want her to be alone if she didn't feel well.

"No," she said firmly. "I want you to stay."

Tessa walked up to us with her keys in her hand. "Here you go. Are you sure you don't want me to take you?"

Bree took Tessa's keys and shook her head. "No. I want to be alone."

"What's going on?" my sister asked.

"I don't want to talk about it right now." Bree gave me a quick glance before turning back to my sister. "Let's just say, you were right. But now is not the time or the place." She smiled slightly at Tessa. The first smile I had seen since she'd disappeared on me earlier. "I'll talk to you later."

Tessa pursed her lips but didn't fight Bree. "Okay," she relented.

Bree turned to me. "I'll...talk to you later too." The way she said it was less of a reassurance, like with my sister, and more of something she had to do out of obligation.

I didn't like how this was playing out, and I wished Bree would talk to me. I felt helpless as I watched her leave. I definitely did not fail to miss the fact that she hadn't hugged or kissed me good-bye.

As soon as Bree was gone, I turned to my sister. "What was that about?"

She shrugged. "I honestly don't know. She didn't say much to me. Just that she needed to borrow my car immediately. You heard the rest."

I crossed my arms over my chest. "You might not know, but you have a damn good idea. What was she talking about when she said that you were right?"

Tessa's eyes immediately shifted away from mine. "I don't want to tell you in case I'm wrong."

"Tell me anyway," I said through a clenched jaw.

"Just stuff about you." She shrugged. "You've heard it before. That you're popular with the ladies. Basically, I told her that you're charismatic and that you might mean more to her than she does to you." She held up her hands. "But that's it. And I said that stuff last week. I've actually changed my mind because when I first got here, I was pretty convinced that the two of you were happy together. What happened?"

I threw my arms up. "I don't have a fucking clue. We were good all afternoon, and then she went to use the restroom and came out, wanting to leave." I rubbed my forehead. "I don't know what to do. She obviously didn't want to talk to me." I sat down at the end of a picnic table and put my head in my hands.

Tessa sat down next to me and put her hand on my shoulder. "I can't believe I'm going to say this because, normally, I believe when a woman wants to be left alone, a man should leave her alone."

My heart sagged in defeat.

"However, I know that Bree likes you. There is no way she would be involved with you after everything she went through if she didn't feel something for you. Something must have happened. And I think you need to go and find out what went wrong."

My hopes rising, I looked up. "Really?"

"Yes."

"Do you think I should wait a little bit? Give her some time alone first?"

"Uh...no. She is only going to ruminate on this. You need to get over there before she gets more in her head than she already is."

I leaped off the picnic table bench.

That was all I needed to hear. I was going to find out what in the hell had gone so wrong.

———

I resisted the urge to pound on Bree's door and burst into her house. Instead, I took a deep breath and knocked politely.

At first, I was almost afraid she wasn't going to answer, but my sister's car was in the driveway, so I knew she was home. Soon, I heard her footsteps.

When she opened the door, I saw the look of surprise on her face. I guessed she hadn't expected me to come after her.

"Zack."

"Do you mind if I come in?"

She hesitated but stepped back and let me through.

"What are you doing here?" she asked, closing the door.

"Something is obviously wrong, and I needed to make sure you were okay."

"But your family..."

"Screw my family. You are more important to me than the people I see once or twice a year."

Her eyes got wide as her jaw dropped open. "I...I didn't know you cared so much."

"Of course I do." I stepped forward and tentatively picked up her hands. "Will you please tell me what is wrong? I want to help."

She sighed. "I heard some of your relatives talking about you in the restroom. They didn't know I was there. And I guess I got scared."

I had a few guesses as to who would be talking about me behind my back, and I gritted my teeth. "Do you know who?"

She shook her head.

"What did they say?"

"Mostly that they hadn't seen you with a girlfriend in years. And that they know you sleep around. And I guess your cousin Jay saw you leave a bar with two women one night." She looked into my eyes. "Zack, I can't compete with two women. And I don't know what I would do if you cheated on me." She looked off into the distance. "I know it's not my fault that my ex-boyfriends cheated on me, but at some point, I have to wonder if there is something wrong with me."

I tugged on her arms. "No way. There is nothing wrong with you. Men...well, men are just assholes. Some are going to cheat on any and every woman they date. And some are too lazy to end a relationship before looking for the next one. Others just plain don't put in the work to keep a relationship good." I drew her closer to me. "But I am not going to cheat on you. I don't want any other woman or women. I just want you. And yes, I used to sleep around, but I have never cheated on anyone in my life."

A small smile ticked up the corners of her mouth. "But what if you feel like having sex with someone else?"

"Then, I will break up with you. But I will not cheat on you. Ever." I let go of one of her hands and ran my thumb over her cheek. "I know you've been hurt and you're scared, and I haven't had a girlfriend in some time, but we don't have to get married right away. Or even move in together next month. We can take this relationship as slowly as you want, so you can trust what we both feel. But I am not going anywhere because I already know I am falling in love with you."

She sniffled, and a tear ran down one cheek. "I am afraid, but I think I'm falling in love with you too."

"*Yes.*" I pumped my fist in the air.

"Zack."

I pulled her close and kissed her. "I can't help it. You said you love me."

She laughed. "I said, falling in love with you. And you said the same thing."

"Okay, I know you had a rough afternoon. We can say *I love you* tomorrow."

She laughed again.

"Does this mean you'll give us a chance?"

"Yeah, I suppose."

Leaning down, I kissed her neck. "I love you, Bree," I whispered. I couldn't wait until tomorrow.

"I love you too," she whispered back.

I took her mouth in a long, deep kiss. "I can't believe you're really mine."

"Me neither." She bit her lip, and a nervous look crossed her face. "I just realized that now, I have to go and tell my mother we're back together."

This time, I laughed. "Don't worry. Your mother loves me too."

Epilogue

BREE

"HOW'S EVERYTHING going with the bakery and coffee shop plans?" Pru asked Tessa and Alexis.

Our two friends exchanged looks, and Tessa cleared her throat. "We actually found a great location that's going to be available soon."

"That's awesome," Isabelle said. "Location is everything, they say."

"Yeah. The only thing is, we've had a little bit of a setback."

"What's wrong?" I asked.

"Tessa's being nice. It's me. I'm the one who has set us back. My ex still hasn't sold our house," Alexis admitted.

"*What?*" several of us asked simultaneously, shocked.

When Alexis and her husband had gotten divorced, part of their decree was, her ex was supposed to sell their house and split the proceeds with Alexis. Their shared home was seven bedrooms, five bathrooms, and over six thousand square feet. Meanwhile, Alexis had been living in a two-bedroom apartment since the divorce. She honestly could afford a slightly bigger home on her own, but she was saving for the store she and Tessa were planning to open. Her half of the house was supposed to go toward the down payment of the shop.

"All is not lost," Tessa said. "I actually signed up with a temp agency to earn some extra money."

"You're going to work two jobs?" I asked in surprise.

I felt bad. I'd been so preoccupied with Zack that I hadn't noticed that Tessa and Alexis were struggling. Although last month's dinner had been crashed by Zack and his friends. It made sense that Alexis and Tessa hadn't wanted to talk about what was going on with the bakery and coffee shop then.

"No. Remember, I put in a six-month notice so that my job would have plenty of time to find a replacement for me. My six months is up at the end of this month. And I can't change my mind. They've already hired my replacement, and I've been training her the last few months."

"I'm sorry," Alexis said.

"Don't be sorry. Your ex is a dick. And at least you still have your job."

"So, what are you going to do?" Elizabeth asked Tessa.

"Not sure. They haven't called me with any positions yet. I just completed my registration with them." She smiled. "But no more talking about this. Let's talk about something fun." She looked at me and wiggled her eyebrows. "Bree has some news to share with us."

Six sets of eyes turned to me, and I suddenly got nervous.

"Spit it out," Pru said with a grin.

"Okay." I took a deep breath. "I know we just started our Man-Haters Club, but, um...I'm kind of seeing someone."

A collective gasp sounded, and Tessa snorted. "*Kind of* seeing someone? She's practically living with my brother."

Paisley, who was sitting next to me, smacked my arm. "The hot one?"

"He's my only brother," Tessa said.

"Yes, the hot one," I answered.

"You know, I didn't expect us all to really stay faithful to this club. But I definitely did not think Bree would be the first to bail," Pru said.

I lifted a shoulder. "It just kind of happened." I pointed my finger at Tessa. "But we are taking it slow. We are not living together. We both still have our own places."

Tessa rolled her eyes. "They spend every night together."

She wasn't wrong, but I still liked to think we were taking it slow. Even if only in semantics.

I shrugged. "I like him, okay?"

"Aww," they said at the same time.

Tessa, who was sitting on the other side of me, leaned over toward me. "I'm happy for you. And just think, when you and Zack get married, we'll be sisters-in-law."

"Whoa. Slow down. No one's talking about marriage yet." I narrowed my eyes, as if in deep thought. "But maybe you're not a true man-hater either." I pretended to gasp. "Who knows? Maybe you'll find someone too."

Tess wrinkled her nose, as if horrified, but everyone else laughed.

"You never know," I teased.

Someone has to be next.

<u>Turn the page for a sample of</u>

NOT ANOTHER BILLIONAIRE

Not Another Billionaire

TESSA

Monday morning, I walked into the tall metal building in the middle of downtown Minneapolis. I'd forgotten to tell my friends that this was the other downfall to the job. Driving around downtown wasn't easy, and parking was almost always a nightmare. My last job had been in a suburb with a nice parking lot attached to the building. Thankfully, there was a parking garage close to the office building, so I didn't have to go too far.

I headed to the security desk at the front. Even though the Bradford Group was a big business, they only used one floor, and the other floors belonged to other businesses. It made me feel a little better about being at this intimidating location.

"Hello. How may I help you?" the polite gentleman in a security uniform said from behind the desk.

"I am starting a job at the Bradford Group today."

He clicked something into his computer. "Your name, please?"

"Tessa Archer."

He scanned his screen. "Ah, there you are. Oh, it looks like you are only here temporarily."

"Yes. I'm filling in as Mr. Crawford's assistant."

The guard's eyes rounded. "Wow. The big man himself."

Oh shit. That didn't seem like a good response. Why was the guy so wide-eyed?

"Yes, the CEO himself." I leaned in. "Is there something I should know before I start my first day?"

The guard shook his head. "Oh, no. I have nothing to say."

That sounded like he had something very interesting to say but didn't want to get in trouble.

I sighed. I hoped I wasn't going to immediately regret this decision. The dollar amount was enticing for my business plans, but I didn't need any workplace drama.

"Okay then. Do I need anything before I go up?"

"One second, please." He shuffled some papers around on his desk until he found what he was looking for. "Here is your temporary pass. Once you're up there, they will take your picture and give you a permanent ID that you can use for the elevators." He waved the white plastic card in his hand. "This will be deactivated after twelve hours, so make sure you get the ID; otherwise, you'll be stopping here again tomorrow."

I held out my hand. "Got it."

The guard slapped the card down. "Have a good first day. And good luck."

"Thanks," I said, heading toward the staff elevators.

Once I reached the eighth floor, there was another reception desk right at the front.

How many people do I have to go through?

The two women greeted me with smiles, and I explained who I was all over again.

"Oh, thank God you are here," one of the receptionists —a blonde woman—said with way too much relief on her face.

Uh-oh. This seemed like another red flag.

The other receptionist—a brunette—clasped her hands together, as if she were praying. "Yes, the last two weeks have been awful."

"Uh...I'm not sure I want to work here if it's that bad," I told them. I was only half-joking.

They bolted around the corner and took my arms.

"No, no, it's not horrible. Let us show you to your cubicle, and then we'll take you directly to HR to get your security badge," the blonde woman said.

"I don't even know your names."

"Oh, I'm Rhonda," the brunette said, "and that's Colleen."

"That's great. I'm Tessa, and I am perfectly capable of walking under my own power."

They both laughed and let go of my arms while I

resisted the urge to spin around and make a dash toward the elevators.

———

After Rhonda and Colleen showed me to my cubicle, they took me by the break room and then HR. I had a new badge that was really just a white rectangle to give me access to the building. When I went back to my desk, it was only after I sat that I realized they hadn't introduced me to my new boss.

I stood up and looked around for someone to give me guidance. Technically, I was out in the main area with the assistants and additional people who didn't get their own private space. But Mr. Crawford's office was in the back and around a corner, so I was secluded from the others and had some privacy.

Mr. Crawford's door was closed, but I could see light coming from underneath, so there was a good chance he was in there. But he might be one of those people who didn't want to be disturbed if their door was closed. One of the lawyers I'd worked with at my old job was like that. We'd all known not to even knock unless it was an absolute emergency.

I finally resigned myself to going back up to the front to find either Colleen or Rhonda when something in my peripheral vision caught my attention.

It was a man wearing a white tank top, a pair of black gym shorts, and a sheen of sweat. He looked to be early to mid-thirties with dark blond hair, styled in a fauxhawk, and a beard.

At first, I thought maybe he was a messenger, but he didn't have anything with him, except a water bottle and a look of determination as he headed for my new boss's office.

I didn't know what to do. Did I let him go? Did he even belong here?

He sure didn't look like he belonged in an office building, but what if he was Mr. Crawford's son?

I had thought of Mr. Crawford as being in his late fifties to early sixties, making this man too old, but I could have been wrong.

And if I only asked him who he was, I couldn't get fired for that. *Right?*

I bolted over to him so fast that he almost ran into me, but I didn't want him to walk into the office, unannounced.

"Hello, sir," I said. "May I help you?"

He took a step back and looked at the door, which was now behind me. "I don't think so. Can I ask who you are?"

"I'm Mr. Crawford's assistant. It's my first day, and I apologize, but I'm unfamiliar with his clients."

I was pretty sure this guy wasn't a client, but it was the politest thing I could call him.

He raised an eyebrow. "Can I get your name?"

I cringed inside. Wanting someone's name was usually a bad sign. He probably wanted it, so he could complain about me later.

"Tessa," I answered reluctantly.

Nodding, he flipped open the lid to his water bottle and took a long drink.

It was then that I noticed this man was built well. Broad shoulders, nice biceps, and I would bet five hundred dollars that he had a six-pack under that tank top of his because his legs were thickly muscled. When I brought my eyes back up, I didn't miss the bulge in the front of his black shorts either. The man was clearly not aroused, yet I could see a faint outline of his penis anyway.

I plucked the front of my shirt. All of a sudden, it felt warm in there.

The sound of the man's water bottle clicking closed jolted me back to the present.

"So, Tessa, did you happen to Google the Bradford Group before you started?"

This felt like a quiz.

"Just a little." I mean, it was my friend, but it still counted, right? "I know this company was started twelve years ago," I said with a smile to show him I had done my homework.

I didn't know who this guy was yet, but he must have some serious clout with my new boss if he was asking me questions like this.

But this guy didn't seem to be impressed with my answer. "Did you happen to look at any images during your Google search?"

Oh no, this guy had to be Mr. Crawford's son. Or what if he's Mr. Crawford's lover? Or best friend?

"No," I finally admitted.

"Do me a favor."

Do I have to?

He raised his brow.

"Okay."

But if he asked me to go and fetch him coffee just to prove he was more important than me, I was out of there. I didn't care how much they planned on paying me.

That was a lie. I would totally get this unknown person coffee if I had to. I just wouldn't like it and would definitely be complaining to my friends later.

"I assume you have a smartphone."

I nodded. "Yes."

"I want you to look up *Bradford Group, Seth Crawford.* And then click on Images."

I pointed over at my desk. "I have to—my phone is—" I cleared my throat and held up my finger. "Give me one moment."

I left my spot that blocked him from entering my boss's office, wondering if he'd make a break for it but he stayed where he was.

I found my phone in my purse and searched exactly what he'd asked me to. Once the search results came up, I clicked over to Images...and was flooded with pictures of the guy standing a few feet away from me, only he had on a suit and jacket on my phone.

My mouth dropped open, and I slowly lifted my gaze to his.

I had royally fucked up because he wasn't Mr. Crawford's son, or lover, or best friend.

"Can I go into my office now?"

He was Mr. Seth Crawford, the big man himself.

I tried to apologize, but only a squeak came out, so I simply nodded.

As soon as he was inside and the door was closed, I collapsed in my chair.

I was going to be fired, and I had barely started.

About the Author

R.L. Kenderson is two best friends writing under one name.

Renae has always loved reading, and in third grade, she wrote her first poem where she learned she might have a knack for this writing thing. Lara remembers sneaking her grandmother's Harlequin novels when she was probably too young to be reading them, and since then, she knew she wanted to write her own.

When they met in college, they bonded over their love of reading and the TV show *Charmed*. What really spiced up their friendship was when Lara introduced Renae to romance novels. When they discovered their first vampire romance, they knew there would always be a special place in their hearts for paranormal romance. After being unable to find certain storylines and characteristics they wanted to read about in the hundreds of books they consumed, they decided to write their own.

One lives in the Minneapolis-St. Paul area and the other in the Kansas City area where they both work in the medical field during the day and a sexy author by night. They communicate through phone, email, and whole lot of messaging.

You can find them at http://www.rlkenderson.com, Facebook, Instagram, TikTok, and Goodreads. Join their reader group! Or you can email them at rlkenderson@ rlkenderson.com, or sign up for their newsletter. They always love hearing from their readers.